SHADOW PLAY
THE RATS

Latin American Literary Review Press

Yvette E. Miller

Editor

SHADOW PLAY
THE RATS

Two Novellas
by
José Bianco

Translated by Daniel Balderston

Latin American Literary Review Press

Series: Discoveries

Pittsburgh, Pennsylvania

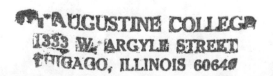

The Latin American Literary Review publishes creative writing under the series title Discoveries, and critical works under the series title Explorations.

Library of Congress Cataloging in Publication Data
    Bianco, José.
        Shadow play ; The rats : two novellas.
        Translation of: Sombras suele vestir and Las ratas.
        I. Bianco, José. Ratas. English. 1983. II. Title.
    III. Title: Shadow play. IV. Title: Rats.
    PQ7797.B53A23 1983   863   83-775
    ISBN 0-935480-11-0, paperback

Cover Design: Kenneth Hamma

Shadow Play was first published in CANTO, vol. 3, no. 4 (1981).

This project is partially supported by grants from the National Endowment for the Arts in Washington, D.C., a Federal agency.

The Latin American Literary Review Press thanks Professor Ronald Christ for his assistance in the publication of this book.

The translator would like to express his appreciation to several friends for their careful reading of the manuscript: María Luisa Bastos, Enrique Pezzoni, John King, Eduardo Paz Leston, Kenneth Hamma, and Josephine Miles, and is especially grateful for the kindness and helpfulness of Pepe Bianco.

Shadow Play and The Rats can be ordered directly from the publisher:
    Latin American Literary Review Press
    P.O. Box 8385
    Pittsburgh, Pennsylvania 15218

CONTENTS

Shadow Play
Sombras suele vestir
[1941]

*El sueño, autor de representaciones
en su teatro sobre el viento armado
sombras suele vestir de bulto bello.*

Góngora

I.

"I will miss him; I love him as if he were my son," said Doña Carmen.

They answered, "Yes, you have been very good to him. But it's the best thing possible."

Lately, when she went to the the tenement on Paso Street, she had avoided the glance of Doña Carmen so as not to disturb that vague somnolence which had become her definitive state of mind. Now, as always, she fixed her eyes on Raul. The boy was rolling up a skein of yarn by winding it around the backs of two chairs; he looked twenty years old at most, and had the astounded expression of a statue, full of grace and indifference. She glanced over from Raul's head to the woman's apron; she observed the four strong fingers bent over each pocket; slowly her gaze reached Doña Carmen's face. She thought with surprise, "Perhaps they were all illusions of mine. Perhaps I never hated her."

And she also thought, sadly, "I will not come back to Paso Street."

1

narrative

There was a lot of furniture in Doña Carmen's room, some of it belonging to Jacinta—the mahogany desk where her mother played complicated games of solitaire or wrote even more complicated letters to her husband's friends, asking them for money; the armchair, its stuffing poking out through the seams. . . . She watched intently the spectacle of such wretchedness. From a distance it looked like a single immutable blackness; little by little friendlier corners appeared (Jacinta knew them well), the clear shadows where it was possible to hide. The misery allowed for some moments of intense joy.

She remembered the period when her brother hadn't wanted to eat. To make him nibble anything at all, they had had to hide a plate of food under the wardrobe, in a desk drawer. . . . Raul got up during the night; the next day the plate was empty where they had left it. So, after eating, while the boy was outside, mother and daughter contrived some new hiding place. And Jacinta recalled a certain autumn morning. She heard cries from the next room. She entered, drew up close to her mother who was sitting in the armchair, pulled her hands from her face, and saw the visage drawn, deformed by laughter.

Mrs. Velez couldn't remember where she had hidden the plate the night before.

Her mother adapted herself to every circumstance with a gay, childlike wisdom. Nothing took her by surprise; every new misfortune found her prepared. It was impossible even to tell at what moment a new mishap had occurred, because it became at once familiar, and what had been a change, an imperfection, was converted imperceptibly into a law, a norm, even into an essential property of life itself. Just as a famous politician and a renowned warrior, conversing in the English embassy, were for Delacroix nothing more than two sparkling fragments of the visible world, a man in blue next to a man in red, so things, as contemplated by her mother, seemed deprived of all moral and conventional meaning; they lost their sting, and attained a kind of metaphysical status, a transcendent purity which made them all interchangeable.

She thought of the secret and slightly ridiculous attitude which Doña Carmen had adopted when she had led her to Maria Reinoso's house. It was an interior apartment. On the door there was a bronze plaque which

2

read: *Reinoso. Commissions.* Before entering, while walking down the long hallway, Doña Carmen stammered out that she thought it would be best not to talk about Maria Reinoso with her mother; Jacinta, glimpsing a trace of innocence in the character of such an astute woman, reflected on the capacity for illusion, on the innate fondness for melodrama of the so-called "lower classes." But—would it really have mattered so little to her mother? She would never know. Now it was impossible to tell her. *she had died*

She began going to Maria Reinoso's. Doña Carmen no longer had to support them all (for more than a year, nobody knew quite why, she had been supplying the Velez family with the necessities of life). Nonetheless, it was not easy to avoid the landlady. Jacinta bumped into her talking to the delivery men in the long hallway, or met up with her in her own room. How was she to be gotten out of there? Besides, thanks to the landlady there was a semblance of order in the three rooms occupied by Jacinta, her mother, and her brother. Doña Carmen, once a week, burst upon the Velezes with the surge of her energy; she opened the doors, and washed the floor and the furniture in a kind of suppressed rage; the shameless mattresses and the doubtful bedding were displayed to the neighbors in the patio. They submitted, half-grateful, half-ashamed. After the storm, disorder began to wrap them again in its snug, hard won complexity.

Jacinta sometimes found Doña Carmen knitting next to her mother. The day Jacinta met Maria Reinoso, Doña Carmen tried to draw her reactions out of her. Jacinta replied in monosyllables. But even the mute presence of the landlady had the power to carry her back to the other house she had just left. And Jacinta, those afternoons, after placating the desires of some man, needed also to placate herself, to forget; she needed to lose herself in the boundless and desolate world which her mother and Raul created. Mrs. Velez played Metternich or Napoleon at St. Helena. She shuffled the cards, covering the table with red and black numerals, with the neckless heads of crowned men and women, clothed in banners, who shared their pathetic, cardboard grandeur. From time to time, without interrupting her game, she alluded to insignificant things the possession of which nobody would have wanted to

3

contest with her, or to the relatives and friends of another era who hadn't been in touch with her for twenty years and perhaps thought her dead. Sometimes, Raul stopped by his mother. Standing with cheek in hand, holding his elbow, he watched the slow progress of the cards with his mother. To distract him, Mrs. Velez made him listen to an affectionate monologue broken by pauses when, panting, her words seemed to stretch and lose all meaning.

She would say: "Let's shuffle the deck. Here is the Queen. Now we can pick up the Jack. In profile, the black-haired Jack of Spades looks like you. A dark young man with bright eyes, as Doña Carmen (who reads cards so well) would say. Let's try again, very slowly this time. At last it looks like we might win a game. That's hard. Will something bad happen to us? Once, in Aix-les-Bains, I was able to pick up all the cards three times in one night, and the next day war was declared. We had to escape to Genoa and take a merchant ship, 'tous feux éteints.' And I kept on playing Napoleon—piling club on top of club, eight on nine—with a great dread of mines and submarines. Where is the ten of spades? Your poor father told me, 'You hope to win so we drown. You always trust in your bad luck. . . . '"

The drug began to work on Jacinta's nerves. The tumult of recent impressions (formed of many atrocious details, discordant among themselves and bringing to bear each its separate witness, its parcel of truth) began to subside. Jacinta felt overwhelmed by exhaustion, which erased the traces of the man with whom she had been barely two hours earlier at Maria Reinoso's; she felt the immediate past—its thousand images, gestures, smells, words—begin to blur, and she became unable to distinguish the boundary between the exhaustion to which she was rather solemnly abandoning herself and that other, the supreme rest. Half-opening her eyes, she looked at her two loved ones, apparitions in that greyness. Mrs. Velez had finished playing. The lamp shone on her inert hands, still resting on the table. Raul was still standing, but the piles of cards, spread out on the yellowing leather, no longer interested him. Doña Carmen was probably at his side, perhaps off to the right. Jacinta would have had to turn her head to see. Or was Doña Carmen at her side? She had the impression of having escaped her, perhaps forever. She had transgressed a line which the landlady could not cross. And the peace she felt became yet more keen, sharp, intimate. In a state of perfect beatitude—head thrown back, neck resting on the chair, eyes vacant, the corners of her lips turned slightly upwards— Jacinta had the expression of an invalid scorched, cleansed by fever, at the precise moment when the fever is dropping and the patient ceasing to suffer.

Doña Carmen kept on knitting. From time to time the motion of the needles imparted a surreptitious, almost animal tremor to the thick ball of yarn at her feet. Like the stupor of stone lions on doorsteps, a globe held in their claws, her indifference seemed somewhat deceptive, as if about to change abruptly into action. Jacinta suddenly noted the room full of hostile thoughts. Doña Carmen and her fellow gossip, Maria Reinoso, were taking control of her once more.

One afternoon, while leaving Maria Reinoso's house, she had surprised them talking by a half-open door. Both became silent, but Jacinta was sure they had been talking about her. Doña Carmen's eyes were small, the iris so dark that it blended into the pupil. When she observed people, they knew they were being watched but could not defend themselves by looking at her in turn, because her opaque eyes cut off that tacit exchange of impressions which is a reciprocal glance. The afternoon that she surprised them, Doña Carmen's eyes were resting; they were wide open and shining, and Maria Reinoso, lifting her anemic face towards the landlady, with her mouth still twisted by the obscene words she had just uttered, addressed those receptive, blank openings.

She did not abhor her encounters at Maria Reinoso's. They allowed her to become independent of Doña Carmen, to support her family. Besides, as encounters they were nonexistent: the silence annihilated them. Jacinta felt herself free and clear of her acts on an intellectual plane. But things changed from that day onwards. She understood that someone was taking note of and interpreting her acts; now the very silence seemed to preserve them, and the eager and distant men to whom she gave herself began to intrude upon her consciousness. Doña Carmen conjured up an image of a degraded Jacinta, united with them— perhaps the true image of Jacinta—a Jacinta created by others who, for this very reason, had no power over herself, but was vanquished in advance by that helplessness which we feel in face of the irreparable. Instead of doing away with that image of herself, Jacinta devoted herself to suffering for her, as if suffering were the only means at her disposal to rescue her; and yet, through suffering she infused that other self with a vexing reality. She abandoned all hope of changing her way of life; she gave up trying. She had begun to translate a book from English, chapters of a partially unpublished scientific work which was appearing simultaneously in various medical journals around the world. Once a week they gave her about thirty mimeographed sheets, and when she delivered a typed translation (she had bought a typewriter at an auction), they gave her as many more. She went to the translation agency, turned in the last chapters, accepted no more.

She asked Doña Carmen to sell the typewriter.

The day came when Mrs. Velez lay among a fragrant disorder of jonquils, spikenard, freesias and gladioli. The local doctor, whom Doña Carmen had pulled out of bed early that morning, diagnosed congestion of the lungs. The funeral service took place in the front apartment by arrangement with the woman who lived there. The tenants entered the room on tiptoe; next to the coffin, they let their glances fall on Mrs. Velez's face with an outburst of what had been suppressed in their footsteps. But these looks did not seem to bother Mrs. Velez. She also bore the whispers of the visitors (seated around Jacinta and Raul), and the comings and goings of Doña Carmen, who distributed cups of coffee, trying unsuccessfully to be quiet, and arranged palm wreaths and fresh bouquets at the foot of the casket. At a certain moment Jacinta broke away from the group, went to the conciergerie, and dialed a number on the telephone.

Speaking in a very low voice, she said, "Has anyone asked for me?"

They answered, "Yesterday Stocker called, asking to see you today at seven. He agreed to call back. It seemed pointless for me to try to reach you."

"Tell him I will come. Thanks."

That afternoon was not easy to forget. Jacinta stayed in her mother's

6

room for a long time with her senses abnormally keen, removed from everything and at the same time highly attentive. She felt withdrawn, and yet the familiar objects there took on a fictive life in homage to her, and shone, displaying their rigorous three dimensions, their internal logic. "They want to be my friends," she couldn't help thinking, "and they are trying to make me notice them." This unexpected display seemed to correspond to the secret identity of the objects themselves, as well as to that of her hidden self. She took a few steps around the room while the taste of coffee lingered on her lips with all the aggressiveness of a strange presence. "And I wasn't even looking at them. Habit cut me off from them. Today I am seeing them for the first time."

And yet, doubtless, she recognized them. There was the extravagant baroque desk (the two piles of cards on the yellowing morocco leather), and behind it a shelf with a built-in mirror. There were her mother's medicines, a flask of digitalis, a glass, a jar of water. And there she was herself in the mirror, her face composed of shifting, mobile surfaces, her features innocent and fine. Still young. But her eyes, of an uncertain grey, were old before the rest of her person. "I have the eyes of a corpse." She thought of her mother's eyes covered by a layer of veined lids, of Raul's eyes. "No, they look different; their looks have nothing in common with mine." The pride of those who are "lords and owners of their faces" showed in her eyes, but already the final verse was applicable to them—"lilies that fester." They had a kind of exceptional insight which takes pride in the fact that it is never used. They reminded her of other people, of someone, of something. Where had she seen that look? For a second her memory was blank. In a painting, maybe. The blank colored itself in with blue and pink tints. Jacinta turned her eyes from the mirror and saw a balcony open before her against a nocturnal background; she saw amphorae, ecstatic dogs, other animals: a peacock, white and grey doves. It was Carpaccio's *Two Courtesans*.

And then there was Stocker, in Maria Reinoso's apartment. He had a worn face and a young, very white body, which his falsely humble clothing seemed designed essentially to protect. When he took it off unhurriedly, carefully folding and stacking each separate piece, he regained the freshness of early childhood. He became more naked than

7

other men, more vulnerable: almost an indifferent child of Jacinta's who caressed various parts of her body without much concern for the human nexus which united them, as one might take objects from here and there to celebrate a ritual known only to oneself and, after using them, return them carefully to their places. His face reflected an almost painful attention: the exact opposite of the desire to forget, to lose himself in pleasure. One would have said that he was looking for something, not in her but in himself; also, despite the mechanical rhythm which he could no longer control, one would have thought him motionless, his expression was so self-contained, introspective, yearning for that shining moment which he hoped would bring the answer to an insistently posed question.

He had recovered his perplexed air. She thought bitterly of returning to the neighbors, the heavy scent of flowers, the casket. But the man showed no desire to leave. He walked about the room, sat down in an armchair, his feet on the bed. When Jacinta wanted to end the encounter, he made her sit down again, putting his hands on her shoulders.

"And now," he said, "what do you plan to do? Is there anyone left to you?"

"My brother."

"Yes, that's true, your brother. But he's . . ."

Although he didn't pronounce them, the words *idiot* and *imbecile* floated in the air. Jacinta felt the need to chase them off. She repeated a phrase of her mother's: "He is an innocent, like the one in Daudet's *L'Arlésienne.*"

And she burst out crying.

She was sitting on the edge of the bed. The bedspread was folded in quarters and, underneath, the sheets, which moments before they had pushed away with their feet, formed a little heap which made her bend forward, hunched up. She stared at the grey rug which covered the floor and disappeared under the bed; in the center of the room it was bathed in light, a very clear grey. Perhaps this very posture caused her tears. They ran down her cheeks, pulling her downwards, gradually making her mingle with the watery grey of the carpet, in a state of dissolution similar to what she had felt those afternoons when her mother played

8

solitaire and talked incessantly to Raul. And then she also felt the light touch of a sweet, penetrating rain on the nape of her neck, on her back. The man was telling her: "Don't cry. Listen: I want to propose something which may strike you as strange. I live alone. Come live with me."

Then, as if answering an objection: "We shall have to understand one another. I hope, I want to believe it possible. Snakes, rats, and owls sometimes share the same cave. What is to keep us from sharing?"

And then, still more insistently: "Answer me. Will you come? Don't cry; don't worry about your brother. For the moment, let him stay where he is. Later on we will see what I can do for him."

"Later on" was the sanatorium.

II.

The suffering of others inspired him with so much respect that he did not attempt to console: Bernardo Stocker dared not put himself at the victim's side and pull him back from the realm of pain. He conducted himself almost like those natives of certain African tribes who, when one of their number falls in the water, beat the wretch down with oars and row away, to keep him from surviving. They recognize a divine rage in the current and the reptiles: how can one struggle with the invisible powers? Their comrade is already condemned: wouldn't aiding him be a sign of a rash desire to prove oneself equal to them? Thus, full of scruples, Bernardo Stocker learned to distrust his benevolent impulses. Later, he managed to repress them. We suffer for our neighbor, he thought, to the extent that we are able to help him. His pain gratifies us with a knowledge of our power; for a moment we are like gods. But true suffering does not admit consolation. As this suffering humiliates us, we opt to ignore it. We reject the generous impulse, and pride, which before made all our faculties serve the heart and opened us to feelings of tenderness, now turns them toward the intellect to find arguments to halt the motions of the heart. We seal ourselves off from the only sadness which, by wounding our self-respect, could truly sadden us.

His impassivity allowed Bernardo Stocker to glimpse the magnitude

9

of another's affliction. However, he reacted instantly to Jacinta's sorrow, in a manner uncharacteristic of him. Was it not due precisely to the fact that Jacinta was not suffering?

Jacinta came to live in an apartment in Vicente Lopez Plaza. That winter did not promise to be especially cold, but when she awoke early in the morning, Jacinta would hear the radiators banging and smell a trace of smoke: Lucas and Rosa were lighting fires in the library and dining room fireplaces. At ten, when Jacinta came out of her bedroom, the servants had already retired to the opposite end of the house.

Bernardo Stocker had inherited this pair of black servants from Tucuman from his father, as he had also inherited his activities in the financial world, his collections of old books, and his not unpraise-worthy erudition in matters of Biblical exegesis. Herr Stocker, of Swiss origin, had come to Argentina seventy years earlier: cattle ranching, commerce, and the railroads were beginning to be developed, the Bank of the Province of Buenos Aires was in the process of becoming the third largest in the world, and the Comptoir d'Escompte, Baring Brothers, and Morgan & Company exchanged shining gold francs and pounds sterling for the government bonds. Herr Stocker worked hard, made a fortune, and each day distracted himself from his work at the Exchange by going to the Foreign Residents Club for a chat, and by the study of the Old and New Testaments. In matters of religion he was a partisan of the spirit of free inquiry, of Christian liberty, and of evangelical liberal-ity. He had participated in the stormy debates on *Bibel und Babel;* he belonged to the German Monist Union; he rejected all dogmatism and authority.

He took a trip to Europe. Bernardo (sixteen years old at the time) accompanied his father on two consecutive nights to the Berlin Zoo. The lay professors, the rabbis, the pastors, and the orthodox theolo-gians interrupted one another in the great hall. They discussed Christi-anity, the theory of evolution, monism, the *Gottesbewusstsein* and the liberating influence of Luther, the Synoptic tradition and that of John. Had Jesus existed or not? Were Paul's epistles doctrinal statements or occasional writings? The nightly roaring of the lions increased the live-liness of the assembly. The president reminded the public that the German Monist Union did not propose to inflame the passions, and asked that they please abstain from displaying their approval or disapproval. All in vain: each talk ended in an uproar of cheers and hoots. Women fainted. It was very hot. On the way out, father and son walked through the Egyptian pavilions, the Chinese pagodas, the Indian temples. They went through the Great Gate of the Elephants. Herr Stocker stopped, handed his son his cane, and wiped his glasses, beard, and eyes with a folded handkerchief. He had sweated or wept; he had decorously contained his enthusiasm. "What a night!" he murmured. "And to think that they talk about a contemporary apathy to religion! The study of the Bible, theology, and the criticism of the sacred texts will never be without its usefulness. Remember that, dear Bernardo. It is useful even if it carries us to the conclusion that Christ did not exist as an historical personality: today we have made him live in each of us. With the help of his spirit the world has been transformed; with the help of his spirit we will transform it still more, and create a new world. Discussions like those today cannot but enrich us."

Thus, accompanied by Christ's spirit and leaning on the arm of his son Bernardo, he went on rambling. They took a cab, left the autumnal woods of the Tiergarten behind them, entered Friedrichstrasse, reached the hotel.

Many years had passed, but Bernardo kept following the footsteps of Herr Stocker, doing everything the latter had done in life. He proceeded without conviction, perhaps, but not for that any the less faithfully. He held that example before him as he might have held any other: circumstances supplied him with it. To tell the truth, it wasn't hard for him to form himself in his father's image. He married young and was soon a widower, like his father. His wife still inhabited the house (strictly speaking, the library desk) in a leather frame. In the morning, in the office, Bernardo read the papers and talked with the clients, while his partner, Julio Sweitzer, took care of the correspondence, and an employee, behind a partition of blue glass, noted the operations of the previous day in the books. Herr Stocker had also modeled Sweitzer in his image. At one time he had been in charge of the accounts, then he became the father's assistant, and now he was the son's partner; he admired them as if they were one and the same person. Don Bernardo,

11

after death, kept coming punctually to the office (twenty, thirty, how many years younger?), clean-shaven and speaking Spanish without an accent, but the substitution was perfect when Bernardo and his present partner (now it was Sweitzer's turn to be called *Don* Julio) discussed Biblical matters in French or German.

At 12:30 the partners separated. Sweitzer returned to his lodging, and Bernardo had lunch in a nearby restaurant or in the Foreign Residents Club: in the afternoon it was usually Bernardo who went to the Exchange. And meanwhile life went on, as the elder Stocker would have said. In the Exchange building on 25 de Mayo Street, men ran from one blackboard to another, deciphering at a glance the dividends of the stocks they were concerned about, and, amidst the din of voices, heard as if in confidence the words which were meant for their ears alone. Around Bernardo they conversed and gestured and jumped about with better or worse luck, but those who had invested in the careful management of Stocker and Sweitzer (Financial Agents, Inc.) could attend to other matters: they could let memories, days, landscapes inform them, and watch the imperceptible miracle of the passing clouds, of the wind and the rain.

Almost every morning Jacinta went to the tenement on Paso Street. Often Raul had gone out with other boys from the neighborhood; Jacinta, when she was at the door getting ready to leave, would see him approaching her with his awkward gait, a little apart from the group, and taller than the others. She came back into the house, this time together with Raul; sitting next to him, she dared at most brush him timidly with her fingertips. She feared she would bother the boy, because he became more aloof the harder she tried to communicate with him. Once, discouraged by such indifference, Jacinta stopped visiting him. When she returned after a week, the boy said to her, "Why haven't you come the last few days?"

He seemed happy to see her.

Jacinta stopped trying to dominate him, and came to feel a purely esthetic need for Raul. Why expect from him the sterile reactions of other human beings, the linking power of words, the radiance of an affectionate look? Raul was simply there, and looked at her without

12

focusing on her. There he was, his forehead flat and tanned by the sun, his wide hands with fingers as separate as those of the plaster casts used as models in drawing classes; his habit of walking back and forth and stopping suddenly in doorways; his skill at rolling up balls of yarn for Doña Carmen. Full of his presence, Jacinta would leave the tenement, and slowly cross the city.

At that hour people had gone home to lunch and left the street quiet. Jacinta, after walking east a while, found herself in a modest, friendly neighborhood of shady streets. And she entered it as if obeying a deep instinctive call. She took one street, turned down another, read the names on the signs. She followed the sloping wall, topped here and there with weathered statues, of the Home for the Elderly, until she came to the end of a somber park; she turned left, resisting the call of domes topped with crosses or excessive marble angels. Suddenly, the sight of a strong, solid house, with a wide entrance and balconies on either side, the paint chipping from its walls, filled her with joy. She perceived a certain spiritual affinity between this house and Raul. Trees also made her think of her brother, especially the trees in Vicente Lopez Plaza. Before crossing the plaza, from the sidewalk opposite, Jacinta made it her own with a glance that embraced lawn, children, benches, branches, sky. The dark, sinuous trunks of the tipu trees emerged from the earth like a contemptuous assertion. There was such force in that petulant impulse, disinterested in everything not involved with their own growth, and, as if as a pretext to justify their height, bound to hold their light, trembling, almost immaterial foliage against the clouds. As Jacinta went up to the third story she observed the pattern of the alternate, green leaflets from closer by. Then she opened the windows and let the fresh air cool off her bedroom.

On the table a thermos of soup and trays of filberts and walnuts would be spread out for her. Jacinta sometimes lingered there; other days she rested a moment, went back down to the street, and took a taxi to the restaurant where Bernardo had lunch.

She would find him with his head bent over the plate, chewing thoughtfully. He would raise his eyes when Jacinta was already sitting at the table. Then, coming out of his shell, he would order her a fancy salad, and pour a glass of wine, in which Jacinta would barely wet her lips.

13

She noticed that these interviews troubled him. They always caught him by surprise. He would try to make conversation, already afraid of the moment they would have to part. He would ask her how she had spent her morning. And how had she spent her morning? She had walked, looked at a green house, looked at trees, been with Raul. He would ask for news of Raul. On other occasions, trying to reconstruct Jacinta's life before he had met her, he would draw a few concrete details out of her which only highlighted the huge desert spaces where both of them wandered lost. For he had the feeling that Jacinta had lost her past, or was in the process of losing it. He would ask her:

"What type of man was your father?"

"He had a beard."

"So did mine."

"My father let his beard grow because he couldn't be bothered to shave. He was an alcoholic."

Yes, these details didn't help much. Jacinta's father was no more than an old failure, like so many others. But Bernardo kept on asking questions, filled now with a feeling of utter futility.

"Did you like to play solitaire as much as your mother? No? Tell me, how do you play Napoleon?"

"I already told you."

"That's true. Three rows of ten cards face down, three rows face up; you put the aces aside. . . . But now that I think about it, it's played with two decks. . . ."

"Let's not talk about solitaire. Only my mother could be amused by it."

"We won't talk about it if it bores you, but one of these evenings, when you feel like it, we'll play together, all right?"

Nor could he get a precise idea of the character of Mrs. Velez. Bernardo was not morally inflexible, and sympathized with the poor old lady. Nevertheless, in order to make Jacinta be more explicit about her, he surprised himself disapproving of Mrs. Velez's habits.

"But—what kind of a woman was your mother? She couldn't have failed to know that you got money somewhere, and if you weren't working or translating. . . ."

"I don't know."

14

"What you are telling me sounds so strange. . . ."

"I'm not telling you anything," responded Jacinta. "I'm just answering your questions. Why do you want to know what my mother was like? Why do you want to know how we lived? We lived, that's all. At first, my mother borrowed money. Later, they wouldn't lend it to her anymore, but she always found someone who helped us through. Toward the end, before I met Maria Reinoso, it was Doña Carmen."

"Doña Carmen is a good person."

"Yes."

"But you hate her."

"I was jealous," answered Jacinta. "I even went so far as to reproach her for having taken me to Maria Reinoso, as if I . . ."

She stopped. Bernardo, blocked by that silence, tried other topics of conversation. Now he attempted to recall their paltry common past.

"Do you remember the first time we met? We always saw one another in the same room. And the last time? I waited for you for a long time, for half an hour, for three quarters of an hour. It seemed you would never come. I think my desire brought you. And even now, I think my desire overcomes you, holds you. I fear that one day you will vanish, and if you go nothing of you will be left to me, not even a photograph. Why are you so unfeeling? You only gave yourself to me once completely. You were helpless. You cried. You were able to move me. Because of that I understood that you were not suffering. That was our last meeting at Maria Reinoso's house."

He looked pathetic. Although Jacinta was barely listening to him, he continued talking: "At Maria Reinoso's you were at least human. You seemed tormented then. Sometime I would like to see you there again. What were the other rooms like? You have been in those rooms with other men. Who were those men? What were they like?"

And, in the face of Jacinta's silence: "I am interested in those men because they have been involved in your life, as I am interested in myself, in that former self, with a kind of retrospective affection. I care about those men as I care about your mother, Raul, Doña Carmen . . . even if you detest her. Hate is the only feeling which lives on in you."

"I would like Raul to go to a sanatorium," said Jacinta.

"To get him away from Doña Carmen?"

15

"Yesterday," continued Jacinta, without answering the question, "I visited a sanatorium in Flores, on Boyaca Street. There are men there like Raul. They walk among the trees, play bocce ball."

"It would be very cold."

"Raul doesn't feel the cold."

Bernardo looked at his watch. It was after three; he had to go back to the Exchange. And he said goodbye with the feeling of having behaved badly. Jacinta would not come to lunch with him again. And so it turned out. A few weeks later, when she came into the restaurant and saw him seated at the usual table, she hesitated a moment. Stepping back, she walked down the hallway towards the door, but was still separated from the street by stained glass windows with the British coat-of-arms. Two people were getting up from a nearby table. Jacinta decided to sit down. But the waiters didn't approach her. They thought, perhaps, that she had finished her lunch. Jacinta waited a while, played with some bread crumbs, then left. Nobody seemed to notice her presence.

That afternoon Bernardo returned home in a cheerful frame of mind. Jacinta was lying down. Bernardo entered the bedroom and spoke to her from the doorway: "I went to the sanatorium in Flores. You can take Raul there. But will he want to go?"

"We will go for him together," said Jacinta, stressing the last word. "You will have to speak with Doña Carmen. Only you can do it."

Bernardo lay down at her side.

"You were right," he said. "The place is pleasant and Raul will be happy there, assuming that we can get him there." (He spoke with his lips glued to Jacinta's neck, almost without moving them, as if trying to turn his words into caresses that could pass unnoticed.) "The director, a very helpful man, showed me the main building and the cottages. We walked through the garden. There are some magnificent magnolias and tall, leafless tipu trees. They lose their leaves before those in our plaza. The garden is a bit overgrown."

Then, without any transition: "The view from the room Raul would occupy is sinister. Those flower beds full of tall, dark grass, those bare branches. All that was missing was a hanged man."

He sat up. All of a sudden he stretched his legs over Jacinta and stood up next to the bed. He straightened his collar and tie, sprinkled himself with cologne.

"Tonight Sweitzer is coming to dinner," he said. "Don't leave me alone with him for the whole evening."

"I won't come to the table."

"Don't leave me alone," he repeated. "I beg you."

"Why is he coming?"

"He wants us to write a letter."

"A letter?"

"A letter about Jesus Christ."

Jacinta didn't understand.

"Oh, if I have to explain it all to you. . . . Well, a play is being performed called *The Family of Jesus*. A Catholic wrote a letter to the papers, protesting that Jesus never had any brothers or sisters. Sweitzer wants to write an answer saying that yes, Jesus had many brothers."

"And is that true?"

"Anything can be claimed. But — why does that surprise you? Haven't you read the Gospels? When you took first communion and studied doctrine? No? In the doctrine classes they didn't teach the Gospels, only the Catechism? . . . And also the book by Renan? What things you tell me! I would never have guessed."

Jacinta's answers were evasive. Bernardo couldn't be sure if it was she who had read the Gospels and the *Vie de Jésus,* or her mother, Mrs. Velez.

"Well, will you come to the table? Tomorrow we will go to the tenement together, but tonight dine with us. I ask it as a special favor. It's all I ask. Will you promise?"

"Yes."

Sweitzer was waiting for him in the library, examining a color print of *The Two Courtesans* in a leather frame on the desk. Bernardo, while welcoming him, reflected on Jacinta's ambiguity. And suddenly he began to be unhappy with himself for letting such things bother him, and his unhappiness showed in a scornful impatience with Jacinta, Mrs. Velez, the Gospels, the *Vie de Jésus.* He released it by gibing at Renan:

17

"It has been rightly said that the *Vie de Jésus* is a kind of Belle Hélène of Christianity. How well suited is that conception of Jesus to the Second Empire!"

And he repeated a sarcastic remark about Renan which he had come across a few days before while leafing through old issues of the *Mercure de France:* "Renan had two great passions in life: Biblical exegesis and Paul de Kock. This priestly vice, which he contracted in the seminary, explains his fondness for a simple style with a light touch of irony, the *sous-entendue mi-tendre mi-polisson;* but he also acquired from Paul de Kock the art of manipulating hypotheses and capricious or abrupt deductions in fiction. Apparently even at the end of his life Renan's wife had to play all kinds of ingenious tricks to tear *La Femme aux trois culottes* or *La Pucelle de Belleville* from the hands of her illustrious husband. 'Ernest,' she would say, 'be good, first write what M. Buloz asked you for and then I will give back your toys.'"

Sweitzer smiled weakly: he didn't find irreverent remarks at all funny. And Bernardo said to Jacinta: "Paul de Kock is a licentious writer."

He listened to Jacinta's voice. She was talking about some English novels she had read; from her words he gathered they were pornographic works published for sailors.

"Their covers were of violent colors, reds, yellows, blues. They were sold on the Paseo de Julio and the booksellers hid them in their portable stalls together with the contraband cigarettes behind a row of wooden shoes."

They went into the dining room.

Jacinta sat at the end of the table. When Lucas came in with the platter there were one too few place settings. Bernardo gestured to him: he could hardly contain his impatience. Lucas had to put down the platter, and come back a moment later with another tray; he set the missing place with an impertinent slowness.

Sweitzer, very confused, took a clipping out of his wallet and some papers written in his old-fashioned hand. "I have sketched out an answer," he said. He began to read aloud:

"The controversial subject of Jesus's brothers is not treated only in Matthew 8:55, as Mr. X seems to believe (here, to be more explicit, I transcribe the other relevant passages in Matthew, Mark, Luke, John,

18

Corinthians, and Galatians). Three theories have been based on these texts: the Helvidian theory to which Mr. X refers, which claims that Jesus's brothers and sisters were born of Joseph and Mary after his birth; the Epiphanic theory, which claims that they issued from an earlier marriage of Joseph; and the Hieronymite theory, to which St. Jerome adheres, which claims that they were children of Cleophas and of a sister of the Virgin also named Mary. This last is the doctrine of the Church, defended by its great thinkers."

While talking he nibbled from time to time on almonds or sliced walnuts and filberts, spread out on a plate to his left. Sometimes, with his hand in the air, he rolled a nut around between his fingers to remove its tawny skin. With the pretext of serving himself, Bernardo moved the plate out of Sweitzer's reach, between Jacinta and himself. Sweitzer looked at him with astonishment. Bernardo asked: "Why don't you quote from the Acts of the Apostles?"

"That's true; after eating, if you will lend me a Bible . . . ."

"No Bible is necessary. Note down: chapter one, verse fourteen: 'These all continued with one accord in prayer and supplication, with the women, and Mary the mother of Jesus, and with his brethren.' Good, that finishes off the preamble. Now, which of the three theories do you propose to accept?"

"The first, obviously. How would you begin?"

Bernardo couldn't resist the chance to show off.

"I would begin by saying," he answered in a professorial tone: "It is true that in Hebrew and Aramaic there is only one word used for the concepts *brother* and *cousin,* but that is not a sufficient reason to twist the meaning of the texts. For Greek, on the other hand, has a wealth of terms: *adelphos* for brother, *adelphidos* for first cousin, *anepsios* for cousin. The community at Antioch was bilingual and there the tradition passed from Aramaic to Greek. Goguel cites a verse from Paul (Colossians 4:10) which says, 'and Marcus, cousin to Barnabas.' If Paul in his other writings speaks of Jesus's *brothers,* there is no reason to confuse the two terms."

He paused, then continued: "There is so much else which should be added. . . . Tertullian accepts that Mary had many children with Joseph. The sect of the Ebionites and the Christian martyr Victor of Petau (martyred in 303) affirm the same thing. Hegesippus says that Judas

19

was a *blood brother* of the Savior. The Didache says that Jacob, Bishop of Jerusalem, was a *blood brother* of our Lord. Epiphanius reproaches Apollonius—who taught that Mary had children after the birth of Jesus—for his stubbornness."

Sweitzer took some notes in his notebook. Bernardo continued holding forth. As he spoke his initial bad humor disappeared. He had found himself again; he was satisfied with his certainty, his memory, his erudition. He received Sweitzer's respectful silence as a tribute. He yearned for Jacinta's approval.

Jacinta sat aloof from everything, vague, distant, as if dispersed in the atmosphere of the dining room. Bernardo stammered, drank some wine, lowered his head; a few pink drops still remained in the bottom of the glass. He raised his head; before his eyes the flames from the hearth danced on the backs of the empty chairs along the wall; the carved cedar boards and Lucas's face flashed with a kind of intermittent vitality, revealing unexpected, reddish shades; and the drops of crystal in the Viennese chandelier seemed to swell, heavier than ever, as if threatening to shatter at any moment on the tablecloth. (It seemed as if Lucas, approaching the table, did not come out of the shadow in order to remove the plates so much as to join that shining circle of human well-being.) But Bernardo had lost the thread of his thought. Trying to recover, he said with some effort: "There are reasons for thinking that in the first centuries of the Christian Era people often talked of Jesus's brothers. Guignebert . . . ."

Sweitzer interrupted, "We have more than enough already. After all, it's only an answer."

But Bernardo added insistently: "Since a Catholic wrote the letter, it would be good to end with a Catholic quotation. Something like this: We should remember the exemplary sincerity of Father Lagrange, who recognizes that historically it remains unproven that Jesus's brothers were his cousins."

He went to sit next to the fireplace, taking his cup of coffee with him. Two big logs burned brightly. He picked out a wavy red flame, the red ocher—almost an orange—of the logs, and the delicate blue tint which flickered from the bed of white ashes. Jacinta was repelled by the spectacle of fire. And he, he would have liked to be consumed like those

20

logs, to disappear once and for all. He moved nearer and nearer the fire, and seemed intent on burning his feet. "I am always so cold." Then, thinking of the others, he rose to half-open a window. Sweitzer, pulling himself with some difficulty out of the armchair, started taking leave.

"Thanks a lot. Tomorrow I will write up the answer. If you come by the office after leaving the Exchange, you can sign it."

But Bernardo answered that he would rather not, and when the other asked him why, answered: "These discussions are useless. And—who knows?—perhaps they foment an error. With every passing day, the humanity (or better, the 'historicity') of Jesus seems more dubious to me."

He paced back and forth across the room, his eyes dry and burning. He went out and came back almost immediately, carrying a nobly bound but moth-eaten book; he opened it, and the spine, coming loose from the brown covers, had to be held with care. Sweitzer read the title: "*Antiquities of the Jews.* Oh, the Havercamp edition. . . . Did you intend to read me the well-known interpolation? Don't bother."

But nobody could have stopped Bernardo. He read the interpolated quotation and, this time rather clumsily, developed the thesis that Christianity predated Christ. He spoke of Flavius Josephus, of Justus of Tiberiades. . . . Sweitzer listened inattentively to his passionate incoherence.

"But that's a completely different matter," he said. "Besides, those arguments have been fiddled with before. And they don't seem very convincing to me."

"I don't base my position on them," answered Bernardo. "My conviction belongs to an order of truth which we come to hold because of feelings, not reasonings."

Then, as if speaking to himself: "I was thinking of the famous story of the painting. . . . How does it go?"

He heard Jacinta say in her monotonous voice: "You know. The painting fell down and we discovered that Christ was not Christ."

"Told in that way it is incomprehensible," thought Bernardo. He told the story himself.

"It was an old engraving, a collage from the colonial period decorated along the edges with wrinkled blue velvet, and covered with a convex

21

piece of glass. When the glass broke it turned out that the image was of a Dolorosa. The long hair and beard had been added with pen and ink, along with the crown of thorns, and the cloak was hidden by the velvet."

He added in a whisper, "Jacinta Velez was just a girl then, and was terribly disillusioned. Her incredulity dates from that moment."

Again he heard the monotonous voice: "No," said Jacinta, "now I believe."

Christ had sacrificed himself for all men, for men who resembled their Redeemer less the more perfect they seemed: strong, wise, complex, keen, dissatisfied, sensual, curious men. And, at the edge of this flock, other beings vegetated in a mysterious state of bliss, freed from reality and scorned by other men. But Christ loved them. They were the only ones in the world with a chance of being saved.

Bernardo said goodbye to Sweitzer. Jacinta thought of Raul. She needed desperately to be at his side, surrounded by trees, in the sanatorium in Flores.

III.

Sweitzer reread Bernardo's letter while riding in the noisy taxi. It was written on blue rag paper, and the letterhead showed the facade of a building with a slate roof and innumerable windows. The letter read:

> Dear Don Julio:
> Recently I have not been able to interest myself in business affairs. Every effort exhausts me. I therefore decided to consult a doctor, and am presently on a rest cure under his supervision. This cure could last several months. Therefore I propose two alternatives to you: look for a trustworthy person to take my place, paying him a suitable salary and a certain percentage of the income which would otherwise be mine, or let's liquidate the firm.

Then, as if to show up as false the phrase in which he alluded to his present disinterest in business affairs, Bernardo made some very sharp remarks, in Don Julio's judgment, about an investment which had not yet been decided. He added, at the end of the letter, "Don't bother to come see me. Answer in writing."

Don Julio would later reflect on this last sentence.

He arrived at the sanatorium, asked for Bernardo, showed his card. They made him wait in a room with big windows which opened on the garden only at the top. After ten minutes a tall man with a ruddy face entered.

"Mr. Sweitzer?" he asked. "I am the director. I just got here."

And he adjusted the straps of his white coat around his wrists.

"May I see Mr. Stocker?" asked Sweitzer.

"You are his partner, right? 'Stocker and Sweitzer,' yes, I know the firm. I had occasion to deal with Mr. Stocker in March, 1926. I remember the date exactly. I had some funds on hand, not much, but Mr. Stocker recommended the second bond issue of the Lignito San Luis Company—I will never forget the name. The shares, in your hands, were sold at a great profit. With that financial base I established my sanatorium."

"May I see my partner?" insisted Sweitzer.

"Of course, Mr. Sweitzer. Mr. Stocker is not a patient here, as you know. He came to the sanatorium bringing a boy he was concerned about, Raul Velez. There is a kind of peaceful atmosphere here which must have seduced him. One day he appeared with his bags. He told me, 'Doctor, I have decided to take a rest and come here also. But keep it a secret. I don't want to be bothered; I don't want to speak with anyone, not even with the doctors.' You must be the only person to whom he has given his address."

"He wrote me."

"We have put him in the last cottage, the most isolated one. Mr. Stocker is in one room, Raul in the other."

He hesitated a moment.

". . . This boy is a sad case," he went on. "We doctors are discreet, Mr. Sweitzer. There are things which we don't have any reason to know, which we don't want to know, but gradually we become aware of certain family circumstances. Anyhow, be that as it may, Mr. Stocker feels a truly *paternal* affection for this boy. Can you tell me why he has delayed

23

so long before entrusting him to a psychiatrist?"

"Is it no longer possible to cure him?" asked Sweitzer.

"It is not a question of curing, but of adapting. Adaptation involves great sensitivity on the part of the patient and of the surrounding environment. An adjustment must be made to the patient, to be sure, but he must also be required to make a slight effort, so that it is he, in reality, who is adjusting to everyone else. We must get him in touch with others. Of course true intellectual communication, such as that between us at this moment, is unattainable, but a basic level of communication is possible. We must have the patient understand and conform to certain patterns of everyday life. Progress, at least, must be made in that direction."

"And now it is too late. . . . "

The other looked at him with distrust.

"It is never too late," he answered. "Raul Velez has only been here in the sanatorium for two weeks. It is difficult to diagnose the difference between hebephrenic-catatonic dementia praecox and mental retardation. In either case, certain physical symptoms are lacking: the patient appears intelligent, but seems to live outside of himself, aloof to everyone and everything. Nevertheless, he is docile, gentle, and apparently affectionate. He needs to be surrounded with kindness, but a firm kindness the limits of which he feels. Now, this boy has been neglected in a regrettable fashion. He was in the hands of an ignorant woman, who doubtless loves him very much, but with a love which does not include the slightest discernment. She yielded to all his whims, and the boy went too far, deliberately plunging into madness. That, for such people, is the line of least resistance. At first, the woman was furious with us. She had the nerve to say that she was going to complain to the authorities, because Stocker had no right to place him in our sanatorium."

Sweitzer, this time, made a gesture of surprise. He asked, nevertheless, "And is that true?"

"It appears that Stocker has not acknowledged him legally. But she had still less right to take charge of the boy. It was a question of an insane person without family or property. Who could take care of him better than Stocker? I spoke with the youth officer and obtained a judicial order naming Stocker as guardian. I barred the woman from the sanatorium, because I got tired of listening to her stories. Now we allow her to come, at the request of Stocker himself. I have acceded, but I'm not happy with the arrangement. Raul Velez must be removed from all influences which could remind him of the disorder in which he used to live, or serve to prolong it."

He stopped.

"I am taking up your time," he added. "You wanted to see Stocker. I will go with you myself."

Following the doctor, who apologized for going first, Sweitzer came to a terrace, went down a fan-shaped staircase, crossed a garden with flower beds bordered by seashells, where there was a large, unkempt lawn; here and there, a magnolia with leaves glazed by the recent rain; other, leafless trees raised their gesticulating branches toward the sky. Sweitzer walked with care so as not to get muddy. Around the garden there were brick cottages, separated from one another by mazes of box-wood.

"I'll leave you here," said the doctor. "Follow straight along this path. Stocker lives in the last cottage on the right."

He came on him suddenly, when he stepped on the threshold of the wide-open door. Bernardo Stocker, however, had seen him coming from afar. He was sitting wrapped in two plaid blankets, one draped over his shoulders, the other wrapped around his legs. "Don Julio, I can't even get up to greet you. This blanket . . . " He scolded him for having bothered to come. "You should have written." Then, looking him straight in the eye: "You were with the director?"

"Yes."

"What a bore he must have been. I sympathize with you."

"Are you cold?" asked Sweitzer. "Do you want me to close the door?"

"No, I have discovered that cold is healthy. I like it."

There was a pause. Sweitzer had forgotten the motive for his visit, or he didn't want to admit it to himself. He was distressed. He searched for something to say, any triviality that would help him through that awkward moment. He recalled the paragraph in the letter—"Don't bother to come see me. Answer in writing"—and resorted to the letter as a pretext to justify his presence in the sanatorium. But he limited himself to repeating Bernardo's suggestions as if they had occurred to him, Julio Sweitzer, at that very moment. It was a little absurd. Bernardo came to his rescue and they began conversing with unexpected ease. Bernardo started talking the moment Sweitzer stopped, and his interlocutor, meanwhile, nodded his head, murmuring "yes," "of course," "it's the best thing," "absolutely." Fearful of a new silence, they didn't believe in or pay attention to what they were saying. Bernardo was the first to fall silent. Sweitzer had caught sight of a tall, strapping boy standing in the company of an old woman on the other side of the box hedge. Suddenly the boy came towards them and, when he reached the hedge, instead of coming around it, followed the path straight through, brushing the branches aside with surprising dexterity. He walked with his eyes fixed on Bernardo. Bernardo looked at him in turn. A slow, deep smile appeared on his face. But an unforeseen thing happened. The wind blew a bit of newspaper to the boy's feet. He stopped a few steps from the two men, picked up the paper, looked at it with the expression of someone thinking, "This is too important to read just now," folded it carefully, put it in his pocket and, turning on his heels, walked away. This time, when he came to the hedge, instead of crossing it he turned and followed the path. The two men lost sight of him.

Bernardo's lips remained half-open. Sweitzer could not contain himself and asked, in a weak, eager voice he barely recognized: "That is Raul Velez?"

"Yes," answered Bernardo. "You see: he approaches me spontaneously. But something always comes between us. This time it was that damn piece of paper."

Then, very hurriedly, in the same tone of voice as before: "I had relations with Jacinta Velez, this boy's sister. She lived in my house for several months. She asked me to look after Raul. Before leaving, she herself chose this sanatorium."

"Before leaving . . . for where?"

"I don't know. We would talk. I asked her questions, exasperated her. One always exasperates those one loves. She left."

"She hasn't written?"

"At the tenement where she lived until her mother's death, I went through everything in the desk and found several letters. But they were

26

letters written by Mrs. Velez which the post office had returned. They were addressed to people whose whereabouts are unknown. The numbering of the streets has changed or doesn't match the addresses on the letters, or new buildings have been built at those addresses. Not satisfied with that, I have seen many people with the last name of Velez. Nobody knows them. However, one man I talked to, older than myself, named Raul Velez Ortuzar, said that in his family there was a nearly mythical character, Aunt Jacinta, to whom his mother used to refer from time to time. It seems this Jacinta was a woman of dubious reputation, who died in Europe."

"But that can't be Jacinta," answered Sweitzer immediately. His investigative spirit was alerted.

"No, but it could have been Mrs. Velez. Besides, he wasn't sure that she had died."

"And you hope that Jacinta will come back?"

"She will come to the sanatorium to see her brother. She loves him very much. Raul's 'autism,' as the doctors say, doesn't bother her. She fancies it a sign of superiority. She tries to resemble him."

"But is she sick?" asked Sweitzer, still more intrigued.

"Sick or not, I need her. Do you think she will come, Don Julio? I used to believe it, but now I doubt everything. Do you believe in dreams, Don Julio? I didn't use to believe either, but lately . . ."

"She appeared to you in a dream?"

"Yes . . . and no. I could only see her feet, as if she were facing me and I were looking at the floor. It's strange how expressive and unmistakable even feet can be. I saw her feet as if I were looking her in the face. Then, when I raised my eyes, I couldn't. Everything dissolved into greyness. Last night I dreamed of that same greyness again. Grey, but sometimes white, translucent. I was in suspense, afraid of waking up. Then, understanding that Jacinta was there, I told her that she had deceived me, had made use of me in order to place Raul in the sanatorium. I implored her to let me see her again. We spoke of intimate things, of ourselves, of a woman of whom Jacinta was jealous. I trembled with rage. But Jacinta mocked me instead of getting angry. She said, noticing my trembling, 'Cold like all men.' Suddenly, she began reproaching me. Once I attributed feelings to her which she despises. I

27

claimed to have seen her cry. That hurt her. 'We don't cry,' she said, alluding to herself and Raul. I made her recall that the tears did not correspond to her true emotional state, that later I had explained it all to her in a reasonable way. My explanations, above all, put her beside herself. 'You played tricks too,' she told me in German."

"She speaks German?"

"Not a word, but I heard her pronounce distinctly: *Auch du hast betrogen!* Then I found myself playing solitaire and, when I was about to uncover a card out of turn, had the sensation that someone was pressing my hand to the table. I woke up."

Sweitzer encouraged him. Jacinta would come back to see her brother. It was the logical thing. There was no reason to let oneself by influenced by dreams.

On these words they parted.

Sweitzer walked absent-mindedly. He took the wrong path and twice found himself surrounded by box hedge in the little patio between the cottages. He couldn't reach the garden he had seen earlier. Finally he found his way and walked among the trees, towards the lighted windows of the main building. Suddenly an imposing, dark mass, darker than the shadows, rose up before him. He stepped back in fright.

"I am not a patient," he heard. "I am Carmen, the landlady at the apartment house. I need to talk to you."

They walked to the fence. She was an old woman with a very upright bearing and white hair. Under the lights, surrounded by swarming insects, by the main gate, Sweitzer observed her: a tall, cylindrical hat, a fur muff and stole (the jaws of the otters sinking their sharp teeth in their own brownish tails). Then he looked for the taxi which was awaiting him. The woman crossed the street; he opened the door instinctively and helped her in.

"I wanted to ask you . . ." his companion said, adopting a whiny voice which contrasted with the dignity of her appearance and seemed insincere, as if she were copying the style of those whose petitions she was used to hearing. "You are a good man. You have influence on Stocker. Let Raul be left alone and allowed to return to the building. I love him as if he were my son."

28

"Then you ought to thank Mr. Stocker for what he is doing for the boy. In the sanatorium they will be able to cure him."

"Cure him?" cried the woman. "Raul isn't sick. He's just different. In the sanatorium they make him suffer. The first night they locked him in. Since the boy missed me, he tried to escape. They beat him. The next day he was all covered with bruises. Raul never falls down. And yesterday . . ."

"What happened yesterday?"

"Yesterday I saw him lying on the ground, his mouth all foamy! And the orderly told me, 'It's nothing, just a reaction to the insulin. A provoked attack of epilepsy.' Provoked! Scoundrels!"

"Doctors know more about these things than we do," Sweitzer protested feebly. "Await the results of the treatment."

"And meanwhile will you take care of the building?" the woman asked impertinently. "I cannot afford to come here in a taxi. Stocker doesn't give me money any more. He used to come in the morning, turn the drawers upside down, take away papers, books, pictures. He told me: 'Raul will lack nothing in the sanatorium, Doña Carmen. And the same will go for you. You have been very good to him. But it's the best thing possible.' The best thing! What nerve that man has!"

Sweitzer lost his patience.

"You don't seem to understand. Mr. Stocker has placed Raul Velez here at the request of the boy's sister, Jacinta Velez."

"Yes, he has said that. I know."

"She is the only one who can straighten the situation out. Unfortunately she doesn't live with Mr. Stocker anymore. Instead of slandering him, you should help him find Jacinta."

Stressing every syllable, the woman answered: "Jacinta committed suicide the day her mother died. They were buried together."

She added, "Look, what Stocker has told you doesn't matter to me. He met Jacinta thanks to me. I introduced her to a friend of mine, Maria Reinoso." And she explained matter-of-factly: "Maria Reinoso is a procuress."

It must have seemed to her that Sweitzer was putting her words in doubt by remaining silent, because she went into a rage: "What? You don't believe me? Maria Reinoso will convince you. You can speak to her any time you like. Right now, for instance."

Leaning forward abruptly, she shouted an address to the driver. Then, settling back into her seat, she brushed Sweitzer's face with her round shoulders. He smelled the moldy fur coat.

"I don't want to speak ill of Jacinta," she continued, "but I never liked her. She didn't resemble her mother, the poor dear, or Raul. I love Raul as if he were my son. Jacinta was proud; she despised the poor. Anyhow, now she's dead. She took a flask of digitalis."

The car stopped. While Sweitzer paid the driver, the old woman started down the long hallway. Sweitzer had to hurry to catch up with her.

A woman of uncertain age opened the door. Doña Carmen said to her: "It's not what you think, Maria. The gentleman has only come to talk to you about Stocker and Jacinta Velez. He wants you to tell the truth."

"Come in. If he's a friend of yours, I will tell him what I know. But he will be disappointed . . ." the other said rather affectedly.

When she walked, her slippers brushed along the floor. She made them sit down, and offered them drinks.

"Are you a friend of Jacinta's, sir?" she asked. "No? Of Stocker's? Ah, a very serious, very distinguished man. He has been coming here for a long time. He met Jacinta here, poor thing, and he sympathized with her right away. They saw one another for a month, two or three times a week. Always at my house. Stocker would call me, and I would give Jacinta the message. The day Mrs. Velez died, Jacinta had agreed to come. It seemed strange to me, but she herself had promised. Stocker arrives, and Jacinta doesn't come and doesn't come. I explain the delay to him. We wait. Finally, starting to get worried, I make a phone call and find out about the tragedy. Stocker was extremely shaken by it. He said, 'Maria, leave me alone in this room.' And he stayed there until very late. He is an emotional man. Then, look at all he has done for that retarded boy. That seems to me like the most generous behavior. . . ."

Doña Carmen interrupted her: "Don't talk about something you know nothing about."

The other smiled.

"She is furious," she said, looking at Sweitzer, "because she can't see him all day long. Carmen, Carmen, it doesn't seem possible! A serious woman, at your age . . ."

"I love him as if he were my son."

"Your grandson, you should say."

Sweitzer left when the dialogue began to get more heated. The streets were empty. The street lights in the center of the avenues made the asphalt gleam like huge pools it would be risky to cross. Then total darkness and then again, in the next block, the appearance of another pool. Sweitzer hardly dared cross it. Thus—hesitating at each cross street, clinging to the walls as an insect would to a leaf—he walked for a long time. Here and there the lighted opening of a vestibule made him stand out in silhouette. He was tired and cold, and unable to warm up. Nor could he stop. His very exhaustion impelled him to keep walking. He came to a plaza and crossed the street. That was where Stocker lived. He looked at the intercom and doorbells. When Lucas came down after a quarter of an hour, in underclothes and covered with an overcoat, he was still pressing the third floor button.

"Mr. Sweitzer!" exclaimed the servant. "The master isn't here."

"I know, Lucas. I had a message for you. I came by the house and took the liberty of ringing. Excuse me for having woken you up."

"That's nothing, Mr. Sweitzer. Come in, don't stand outside. We will go up in the service elevator because I have come down without the keys."

They passed into the kitchen. The servant opened doors, turned on lights. "Now they turn off the heat very early. Since there's nobody here, I didn't light fires in the fireplaces." They came to the hall. Sweitzer invented some message to give him in the name of his partner.

"Your master has written me. He says to send the bills to the office. He will come back any day now."

"But he left me enough money," answered the servant.

"I repeat what he wrote me."

"The master is on a trip."

"Yes, that's true, Lucas."

The servant seemed eager to talk. After a moment he added, speaking with his mouth almost closed: ". . . with Miss Jacinta."

Sweitzer asked him very slowly: "Tell me, Lucas, has she been living here?"

"You know too. . . ."

31

"Are you sure? Have you seen her at any time?"

"Seen her, what you can call seeing her . . . I met her once at the street door. It was after lunch. She was leaving the apartment at the moment I was entering. I recognized her immediately."

"But if you had never seen her before . . ."

"That doesn't matter."

"What was she like?"

"She had grey eyes."

"And how did you know it was she?" asked Sweitzer.

"I knew it right away," answered the servant. "She looked at me smiling, as if to say, 'You have finally caught me!' but in a nice way. She seemed to tell me, 'Thanks for the soup and the salad which you prepare for me every day, for the filberts, for the walnuts! Thanks for your discretion!' She is a very kind woman."

"But you never saw her inside the house?"

"They took so many precautions. Until they left in the morning, we couldn't clean the bedroom. In the afternoon, the master was always the first one to arrive. He would lock the hall door. When he opened the inner door the lady was already in her room. Mr. Sweitzer, do you remember the last time you came to dinner? The master was very excited; he wanted Miss Jacinta to join you, he wanted to introduce her to you. While I was setting the table, I heard his voice: 'Jacinta, I beg you. Don't leave me alone tonight.' He waited for her all the way through the meal. Do you remember, Mr. Sweitzer, that he made me set three places? But Miss Jacinta didn't appear. She is a very discreet person."

"In a word, you never saw her inside the house."

"As if it were necessary to see her!" exclaimed the servant. "Now I don't bother to prepare the cold soup any more—ask Rosa—even though the master ordered me to leave food out the same as before. But now she isn't here, I know it, just as I know that before she was living in this house for more than three months."

Sweitzer repeated: "But you never met her inside the . . ."

And the other, insistently: "As if it were necessary to meet her! And the smell? Listen now, Mr. Sweitzer, I wouldn't want to offend you, but Miss Jacinta didn't have that unpleasant smell that white people have. Hers was different. A fresh smell of ferns, of shady places where there's

32

some still water, maybe, but not completely still. Yes, that's it; in the vault, when we go to the Protestant cemetery, there's the same smell. The smell of water beginning to settle in the vases of flowers."

Sweitzer was going to bed. "I haven't eaten this evening," he thought, as he put on his flannel nightshirt. He huddled up in bed, hunted for the hot water bottle with his feet, closed his eyes, stuck out one hand, turned off the light. But the room remained brightly lit. He had left on the chandelier on the ceiling, a bronze fixture with three sharp, pointed arms from which little flames of gas had issued before it was converted to electricity. He got up. When he passed the wardrobe he saw himself reflected in the mirror, shorter than usual because barefoot, his double chin quivering. He rejected this far from seductive image of himself, turned off the light, felt his way back to bed in the dark; then, hugging his shoulders through the nightshirt, he tried to sleep.

The Rats
Las ratas
[1943]

I.

Our house was less quiet than usual. Some friends of the family visited us in the afternoon. My mother was very talkative in their presence, and the visitors, on leaving, must have thought her a bit frivolous. Or they may have thought: "You can tell that Julio wasn't her son."

Julio had committed suicide.

From my room I heard my mother's voice mixed with so many strange ones. Sometimes, when I went downstairs to greet them, the visitors seemed stupefied by certain not exactly uncommon acts: that I could shake their hands, answer their questions, go to school, study music, be fourteen years old. "He's already almost a man," my parents' friends said. "How big he is, how grown-up! What a consolation for poor Heredia!" No sooner would they allude to Julio's death, and when they were about to repeat various sensible commonplaces about the transience of all things human and the inscrutable designs of Providence, which takes from us those who would best have been able to cope with life, this terrible trial, than Isabel would change the subject, answering the disturbed looks elicited by her incoherence with innocent smiles.

The four of us ate the evening meal in silence, my parents, Isabel, and I. After dinner, I walked Isabel home. In the dark street, beneath the indistinct foliage of the trees, I strove to walk at the same pace as she did, and at times, pricking my ears, was able to pick out the barely perceptible sound of the cane which she used to help her walk. Sometimes, without letting go of my arm, Isabel stopped suddenly and poked the tip of her cane in the fresh patches of bark of a plane tree whose old bark was peeling. They were tiresome walks. One night I asked Isabel to intercede with my parents so that they wouldn't send me to school (classes started in April), because I wanted to stay home and study the piano. Another night, Isabel referred to the death of Julio— for the first and last time in my presence. The event itself, more than saddening her, seemed to raise her distrust, her aversion. "It is an act which doesn't represent him," she stammered, as if Julio, by voluntarily ending his life, had arrogated to himself an undeserved privilege. What had he wanted to prove by killing himself? That he was sensitive, scrupulous, passionate? That she was always mistaken? Now, while I write these pages and remember her words that night, I evoke her—and Julio also. I see them forming a kind of monstrous Pietà, and Isabel, ill-humored, baffled, not knowing what to do with the corpse of her nephew which they have placed in her lap, wavering between hurling it away and renouncing her convictions.

We came to the door of her house. It was a dark, two-story house on Juncal Street. I wanted to leave.

"Yes, you had better go," said Isabel. "I don't want to have problems with your mother."

She kissed my forehead, and added, "Your mother is an extraordinary woman. You should be kind to her, help her in every way you can."

At that time I didn't like to hear talk about my mother. Once, surprising her alone after the death of Julio, I found her so undone and overwhelmed, with that expression of false sweetness which sorrow imparts to the face, that I couldn't make a gesture or articulate a word of consolation. The visitors had already gone. My mother, who no longer had to be carefully, explicitly polite, returned to her grief, re-entered her normal state. And I adjusted my conduct to my mother's attitude, tried to "be kind to her" by making her game easier, keeping out of her way, addressing her only when necessary, with the care of an actor who tries not to disturb the harmony of the performance, and limits himself to delivering his lines at the right moment. In this family drama, I fancied myself a secondary character who also acts as director. I believed myself to be the only one who really knew the play. I was in possession of many more or less minute circumstances, and of a not so insignificant, perhaps even decisive, fact, the importance of which escaped the others.

II.

These pages will remain unpublished forever. Nonetheless, to write them I need to think of a reader, a hypothetical reader, interested in the events I am going to recount. I need to start from the beginning.

My name is Delfin Heredia. In me, as in all men, inherited traits are accumulated. Therefore, while recounting a succinct history of my family in this chapter, I will speak of other Heredias who were born or died before me, but who still subsist in me, so to speak, in their most negative form. I will speak of their faults, of my faults. It will be a manner of condemning the race to save the individual, of freeing myself of their faults and of mine at once, of killing them off—irrevocably.

The first Heredia who came to Argentina had been born in Spain, and was doorkeeper of the monastery of San Francisco. As is well known, Canon Aguero was closely linked with the Third Order. During the tyranny of Rosas he took refuge in the monastery before fleeing to Montevideo; on the fall of the dictator, when they named him chancellor of the National College, it is perhaps due to the influence of the Franciscans that he gave the doorkeeper's son a free place in the classrooms on Bolivar Street and, later, a scholarship to the seminary which the Jesuits had founded in Rome for Latin American youths of deep-rooted vocation. After finishing the novitiate and before ordination, the students were granted sufficient means to travel. Delfin Heredia received, in this way, that double culture which includes a Jesuit education (thanks to which humanism has survived in the nineteenth century) and contact with the great cities of Europe; but this hope of the

37

Argentine clergy felt uncertain at the eleventh hour, and returned home without being ordained.

The Franciscans didn't resent his defection. With their help, Delfin Heredia entered the Law School, got married, had two children (Isabel and my father), and was always a good friend of the Church—especially of the Franciscans, his former protectors, and of the Dominicans. Many brown habits and black hoods passed through the house on Juncal Street the day of his death, by the copies of famous pictures which crammed the walls. However, and I want to stress this detail, Delfin Heredia was essentially a patriot, a liberal Argentine, a disciple of Father Aguero and, through Aguero, of Rivadavia. In his last years, the Supreme Court awarded him *otium cum dignitate:* during this period he was credited with the authorship of some of the anonymous articles which most effectively supported the anti-clerical measures of the governments of Roca and Juarez Celman (the expulsion of the papal nuncio, lay education, the law of civil matrimony), and of those making fun of the attacks on these measures by the religious press. Another anecdote: on his deathbed, when they were administering the holy oils, Isabel had to smooth out the wrinkled sleeves of his nightshirt to cover up the Masonic insignia tattooed on his forearms.

My grandfather left behind many debts. The house on Juncal Street belonged to his first child, his daughter Isabel, at that time already the widow of a merchant named Urdaniz. The second child, Antonio, after passing the bar, departed for Europe to study painting. Isabel urged him to return; eventually, she got him to come back from France with a trunk full of canvases, which, with the single exception of a self-portrait, could only be appreciated by the walls of the attic of my house (because they always hung there, backwards). In Buenos Aires, following his sister's advice, he got married (I was born of that union) and obtained a post as an assistant district attorney. I should add that Antonio Heredia brought an illegitimate son back with him from Europe. Julio was ten years old when my father got married.

These circumstances make Isabel's influence on my family understandable. The image of Isabel is not easy to evoke. To give an idea of her physically I have to describe her character, but—although the faces of those we know are made up of successive expressions that modify the

38

features where they alight for a moment and convert them into vehicles of something behind them, making them more invisible the more intensely they are looked at, until we no longer perceive the sparkle of the eyes, the curve of a nose, the expression of a mouth, but rather candor, bitterness, wickedness, sensuality, intelligence—in Isabel the material framework which allows us arduously to reconstruct a face in our memory seemed reduced to a minimum. Her eyes kept guard from deep inside the sockets, covered with blue veins, which she carefully powdered; they were probably bright, like Julio's, but they looked dark. That is to say, her eyes were bright, and her very intense, almost black, glance gave her face the pallor of a ghost. This ghost gave a fright to her husband more than once. Mr. Urdaniz, up to the day of his death, tried never to interfere with her awe-inspiring missions. That is not strange, because Isabel had that imperious spirit which inhibits others, that force of conviction which disregards acts and words. Sometimes, when she intrepidly resisted common sense, I felt ashamed for not knowing how to pierce her arguments, or find them false or superficial. Isabel was always exactly right, whatever her reasons were. Not in vain was she an Heredia, and daughter of a man who came to preside over the Supreme Court—for nineteen days. At Isabel's house there was a genealogical tree of our family: near the bottom was the coat-of-arms, sustained by a Hercules. The lineage of the Heredias, after spreading out victoriously over the Iberian peninsula, begot discoverers and conquerors in the New World; a twig on the Cuban branch, returning to Europe, crossed the Pyrenees: José-María de Hérédia figured in it; my grandfather figured in the Argentine branch. Once I referred to the genealogical tree. "Your grandfather was the son of the doorkeeper of the monastery of San Francisco," my mother commented. It was true, but my mother's words could not contest the new truth which had come from the world of Isabel, that rash, assertive world, imbued with magic, where things seemed true by virtue of the sole fact that they were there. With the years I have had to resign myself to the idea the *The Drunkards* and *The Death of Adonis* are in the Prado and the Uffizi, and not in Isabel's house, but I confess that I destroyed those unfaithful, laborious copies (nobody would buy them) with the pride of a man who frees himself of his material possessions and turns the act of giving up riches into priceless, new riches.

Isabel left behind many letters and notebooks—which abound in moral reflections and paragraphs copied from her reading. She had, perhaps, some talent as a writer (a second-rate writer), and an intellectual dilettantism which moved her to be momentarily enthusiastic about contradictory propositions. For example, among her papers, in a file labelled *Hyacinthe Loyson* in her handwriting, I have found the much-rewritten draft of a letter to Father Hyacinthe.[1] "I cannot admit that your marriage is Christian," writes Isabel to the eminent apostate. "There is only Christian marriage, in the image of that which links Christ with his Church, when neither the man nor the woman have sworn in a solemn oath before God not to marry. You had so promised, dear friend, and now you have broken your promise; you have fallen into the most baleful of the errors of Luther. Alas and alack! The Catholic Church prescribes celibacy to its ministers for such undeniably sage reasons," etc., etc. In the file, after the letter, I found a receipt from the publishing house Coni, dated around the same time, from which I infer that Isabel paid for the new edition of a little book entitled *Observations on the Drawbacks of Clerical Celibacy* (Buenos Aires, 1890), printed first in London, which the ecclesiastical authorities did not allow to be brought into the country in 1816 when it was ordered by Doña Melchora Sarratea. Isn't it curious that every idea should provoke in Isabel a simultaneous affirmation of the opposite idea, and that she should render homage—secret though it may have been, as in this case—to the very principle that she appeared to censure? But this explains how a woman who was in a certain sense so impartial could impose her opinion, because she carried the idea of free judgment to the extreme of not sharing, at bottom, her own opinions.[2] Nevertheless, I wasn't fair to her when I was a boy and had to accompany her home. Isabel, who suffered from insomnia during that period, received visitors at all hours of the night: the street door stayed ajar, the staircase lit; a doorman, posted in the entrance, practiced his profession of idleness. There were various old men who wandered around at night, old friends of Mr. Urdaniz, who came by to visit her after finishing their games at the club. This posthumous homage to Urdaniz, in the person of his friends, had the virtue of astonishing my mother. Many times I have heard her say: "And to think that she never paid any attention to the poor man while

1. It is included in the volume *Du sacerdoce au mariage* (Rieder, Paris, 1927).
2. Isabel differed with Father Hyacinthe about whether or not the latter had been married as befits a Christian, but she never denied him her financial aid. Albert Hou-

40

he was alive, except to pester him." Then, as if giving the explanation herself, she added softly: "It is the fruit of remorse."

My mother had been orphaned at a very early age. She was in a school run by nuns when Isabel brought her to live with her. Some years passed. Suddenly, Isabel began to contemplate the possible return of her brother to Buenos Aires. Antonio, like all the Heredias, had an uncommon artistic gift. Those copies which hung in her house (one had to know a great deal about painting to be able to distinguish them from the originals) had been painted by Delfin Heredia in his youth. Antonio had inherited the artistic temperament of the family. He painted, just as he might as well have written or composed music. He had talent, great talent. That was precisely the trouble: for that reason he never became a true painter. In his paintings he tried to express everything at once. When an artist tries to express everything at once, he often ends up leaving out what is most fundamental: he doesn't commit himself; he runs the risk of spreading himself too thin, of losing himself. Her brother lacked a sense of limits. He also lacked that ingenuous dullness which allows a work of art to be finished after being conceived. He was too intelligent. She didn't mean that artists are necessarily stupid. But taking a hobby for a vocation, playing one's future on a single card, and a mediocre one at that . . . It was lucky that her brother could at least come back home and work. She would always lend him her support.
. "Before Antonio arrived in Buenos Aires, I was sure that I would marry him."

My mother tells me these words. Now, after so many years, I make use of the rare moments of intimacy between us to ask her questions about the past. My curiosity pleases her. I insist: "It must have been painful to be united to a man you barely knew."
"I discovered my duty in the fact that it was painful. Perhaps this attitude had been instilled in me by the nuns. Besides, I took Julio's side. In that respect, your father was firm. He came back from France, to be sure, but he brought his son with him. When we were first married, your father and I continued living with Isabel. They placed Julio in a school in Ramos Mejia, as far as possible from us. On weekdays,

tin, in the second of the three volumes of his erudite apologia (*Le Père Hyacinthe, réformateur catholique*, Paris, 1922), mentions her among "the anonymous benefactors who generously supported the first Gallo-Catholic church in Paris."

when I went to visit him, I found him completely alone in the playground. He still didn't speak Spanish well; he couldn't even say his own name. I taught him to pronounce the *J*. I wanted him to be called Julio, as if he were an Argentine. On Sundays, after lunch, we went to the Casino. We always sat in the front row. The magician pulled doves or piles of cards out of Julio's ears. We were happy."

"You never took me to the circus."

"Poor Julio," my mother went on. "I know that you two didn't resemble one another at all. Julio had different eyes, voice, interests. Is there anything more different from a man of science than an artist? What relation is there between biology and music? I relate them, nevertheless, and your piano, for example, that piano where you study with such fury sometimes, reminds me, I don't know why, of the image of his rats. The likeness is not physical, or intellectual. You coincide in something deeper: your characters."

I assert that my character doesn't resemble Julio's.

"Julio could have been thought egotistical," my mother answers, "but he was unselfish, sensitive; he couldn't bear the suffering of others. Even now, to praise him, I am thinking of your qualities. . . . When Julio died, I felt responsible for his death. In our last talk I told him mean, stupid, inexact things. I told him he was just like Isabel."

"Leave poor Isabel in peace."

My mother doesn't pay attention to the interruption.

"After Julio died, I felt guilty, alone. But then Isabel asked me if it would bother me if you were to play the piano again. She told me you were working at Claudio Nuñez's house, but had spoken to her: together, you had agreed that you should abandon your other studies to devote yourself to music. I answered that the noise of the piano did not bother me. That was false; as soon as I pronounced those words, I began to hear the silence of the piano. At night, remembering the works you played before, the idea of hearing them again tormented me. But the next day the sound came out of the piano less aggressive than I had expected. You were playing exercises, scales, arpeggios. And there was an evident desire to comfort me in the appeal of the piano. I had the feeling that you were addressing me, that you were telling me something very intimate in the only way you could. I began to observe you with more attention,

42

to notice that likeness with Julio which I mentioned. I began to feel less alone."

My mother has gotten wrought-up little by little. I find her aged, worn out. I remember that she has very high blood pressure; I think about her health. Besides, a long time has passed. Her words, which in another period would have made me happy, come too late. My mother insists that these memories have lost all power to hurt her; she wants to keep on talking. But I make her stop.

III.

She who found consolation in my tedious musical exercises has become, over the years, this grey-haired old woman, bent over and happy. Now the tenderness I feel for my mother includes a large dose of pity; as much or more pity than in those already distant times, when pain, imparting a certain splendid stiffness to her, seemed to illumine the last sparkle of youth in her face. I think of Julio's death. The truth is that Julio, before dying, was also the only person who could pull my mother out of her listlessness.

We were living in a house belonging to Isabel on Tucuman Street. I like to remember its facade, with heavy moldings between the windows, and the inner rooms of the upper floor; from there one could catch sight of the magnolia of the Miro Palace, the ceiba trees in Lavalle Plaza, and, in the foreground, lowering one's eyes, the roses, gardenias, and laurel of a small garden. Isabel had the ceilings painted white, changed the coal-burning heater for a deep hearth where firewood could be burned, and built a cluster of rooms at the end of the garden: Julio's apartment. Many of the alterations were only completed when we were already living on Tucuman Street. Suddenly, as I write these lines, I remember my mother's coming and going among the workers, determined in vain to save some plants. The poor woman looked sadly at her shrunken garden.

Ah, I cannot speak coldly of the house where we lived. It weighs on me the same as a character in this story, no less reserved than the others, and eludes every attempt at objectification. To evoke it I have to slip

43

into it until reaching its vulnerable points, the places in the house which are least able to defend themselves from my memory. In a certain sense they belong to me: the gallery upstairs, for example, with its boards dried out and cracked by the sun; near the roof, above the windows which open to the garden, there is stained glass of grey and blue diamond-shaped panes. Many afternoons I would listen to my mother talking with the gardener from that gallery; afterwards I would hear Julio's footsteps as he came in from the street. Then, leaning out a little behind the perfumed tangle of jasmine, I would see him advance and join them. Julio would ask the gardener about the results of a new mixture he had prepared for dusting the roses. My mother would consult Julio about her plants: that year the nasturtiums hadn't produced yellow or purple flowers as usual, but orange ones with red stripes. What did Julio think about planting a couple of ornamental fruit trees, plums or cherries with double flowers, against the dark background of the ivy? Would they have enough space to grow? Later the gardener would leave; my mother and Julio would remain, sitting on a bench. Inside the house some lights were on, scattering yellow rays across the lawn. They kept on talking. I shouldn't say what they talked about, and wouldn't be able to, anyway. They exchanged banal, ephemeral words, now precious and irretrievable for this very reason. The little events of the day sufficed for a dialogue from which I felt excluded; which subsists in me, above all, because of the affectionate tone of the voices. The blue and grey diamonds in the gallery, the perfume of the jasmine have shared these innumerable, fleeting evenings with me, when I remained standing, staring at the mosaics, with my ears pricked, until my mother went into the house and Julio climbed up to his laboratory.

Julio worked in his laboratory in the morning, and in an institute of biochemical research in the afternoon. It was difficult to see him except at mealtimes. Nevertheless I would venture to say that I saw him every afternoon, while playing the piano. Because another place in the house was also mine: the hall. The daylight comes through the skylight, falls straight down on the scores open on the music stand on the piano, and illumines an oil painting behind the piano. It is a self-portrait of my father, I know, I have always known that, but it doesn't look like my father. The person in the painting, seated in a white chair, wears a straw hat pushed back, and holds a pair of gloves in his hands, which are holding a cane. In the background some green leaves, a wall are visible. The canvas is almost bare (wrinkled, its texture imitates the wall, the chair, the gloves), and the painting only acquires something like depth around the tense, burnished face of the model, who is none other than Julio, the only young man in the house. A lock of blond hair falls over his forehead, and the eyes stand out hazel and smiling, among a confusion of eyelashes and dark brows.

How has this self-portrait, which my father painted thirty years ago when he was about Julio's age, ended up in the hall?

IV.

It seems inopportune for me to talk of my accomplishments in this account. I will say, however, that at the age of thirteen I presented myself for examination at a conservatory of music where I was not a regular student, and obtained the first prize and a diploma. Isabel, to celebrate my triumph, gave me an Erard concert grand. I remember her observing with the farsighted person's squint and vague gesture the effect that the vast surface of mahogany made in the hall. She went up to the attic, picked out a painting from the many that were there, and hung it behind the piano. During that period I was working on Liszt's Sonata. I had undertaken it at the insistence of my teacher, and because of one of those puerile ideas that assail us, we never know quite how or when, I associated this piece of music with the piano I had just been presented with and, in a certain sense, with my whole future as an artist. To Isabel's great surprise I had resolved not to open the new piano until I could play Liszt's Sonata on it impeccably. It was too hard a piece for me at that moment. I analyzed its difficulties, taking apart the most arduous passages, which I repeated incessantly; I succeeded in playing them clearly one by one, but when I wanted to put them all together I had to slow down or listen, pale with rage, to an over-dramatic performer who drew forth muddy chords and wrong note after wrong note from the keyboard.

"Play the allegro up to tempo and don't worry about making mistakes," Claudio Nuñez, my teacher, told me, his words of encouragement sometimes drifting into French. His arguments were so specious that he seemed to be making fun of me. "What importance do the wrong notes have?" he would go on. "Elle a quand même du chic, ta façon de trébucher. You have learned how to make mistakes; you are already a true pianist. That is the secret."

Claudio Nuñez had lived for many years in Europe, where he was the teacher of some famous concert pianists. During the First World War he took a trip to Buenos Aires, bringing a letter to Isabel among other letters of recommendation. Isabel proposed that I take some lessons with Nuñez. We told Mlle. Lenoir, my teacher at the time, that I intended to rest for a couple of months, and Mlle. Lenoir contributed unintentionally to my changing to the new teacher for good. When she came back to the house after two months, she was astonished at my improvement.

"Delfin," she said, "today you have played better than ever before. The rest has done you a lot of good."

"It's not the rest," exclaimed Isabel, who was watching the scene. "It is Claudio Nuñez, a good teacher."

Mlle. Lenoir was very fond of me; she searched for a reply, without luck. Suddenly she left the room. I tried in vain to stop her: I saw her running through the garden, crying, talking to herself.

She never returned.

"You were wasting a prodigious amount of time with that imbecile," said Isabel by way of sole comment.

Claudio Nuñez had noted the weak side of my playing. As a first measure, he forced me to play with the whole body relaxed, teaching me that articulation of the elbow and shoulder which demands a strength and flexibility of the whole arm, which I had reserved up to then for the hand and wrist. In this way I succeeded in using my fourth and fifth fingers with the same force as the others. In phrasing, Nuñez made me put constant pressure on all my fingers so as not to lose any detail of the melody. I should add that the lessons took place in an atmosphere of almost frantic optimism, because I learned all of Nuñez's instructions with extreme quickness; all that remained of the difficulties

46

was the pleasure felt on overcoming them. Soon I myself was astounded by the purity which I achieved in the scales, the sonority of the fortissimos, the polyphony of double notes struck simultaneously. And to think that such exquisite, immaterial results were due to little tricks which were relatively easy to learn, like the full rotation of the hand on the arpeggios, or the attack on the fortissimos from close up, filling the chords out by bearing down through the shoulders with the whole weight of the torso, or passing from the thumb to the index finger in series of thirds. Nuñez always repeated that it was essential to enter fully into the music and to acquire the requisite technique from the work itself, be it Bach or Chopin, Beethoven or Liszt. Little by little I abandoned the thankless school of Isidoro Philipp, of whom Mlle. Lenoir was a student, who recommends unmusical, tiresome exercises "to be on one's fingertips": I had acquired that system which consists of an intelligent strengthening of the muscles and tendons of the arm and hand, and which allows us to hold onto our technique even though we may not play for several weeks. I owe it to a thin, authoritarian man with restless lips and a distrustful look. Mentioning him in this chapter, I want to make known my gratitude to him. The years have gone by, but there is nothing about him that I don't remember with fondness. Even his fickleness, his obsequiousness, his unscrupulousness; even his bad breath, which at the time did not greatly amuse me, since in his moments of fervor, to repay me for the pleasure which my progress brought him, he was in the habit of squeezing me in his arms and kissing my cheeks.

I return to Liszt's Sonata. Few pieces have demanded that I work harder. I even got depressed, distrusted my ability, lost my excellent memory for music. Sometimes even such unlikely things happened to me as getting stuck on a certain tonality, prisoner of it forevermore. I desperately sought the right modulation, but couldn't go from the D to the E, and in the third movement, on finishing the più mosso, I found myself repeating the allegro energico of the first part. It was as if the sonata had cast a spell on me. I got up from the piano.

Nuñez stood off at a certain distance, and as a rule didn't interrupt the execution of the lesson. I told him, shaking, while walking around the room: "You see the things that happen to me. It's hopeless."

47

Nuñez, smiling, tried psychoanalytical explanations which had the power of infuriating me: "Basically you are tormented by the octaves of the first allegro; that is why you have played them again: it was an order of your unconscious. And this time you have done better. Now, try again, and remember: keep your wrists rigid, use a lot of forearm, and bear down with your shoulders."

As he spoke these words he struck me hard on the back, and taking my arm dragged me back to the piano.

Several days passed. I still didn't dare play the sonata on the Erard. One afternoon after tea, finding myself alone in the house, I climbed up to the hall as if walking in my sleep, sat down at the new piano, and attacked the first measures of Liszt's Sonata. The tone, very different from that of the old Steinway in the living room, deeper, more velvety, and at the same time less strident, allowed me not to hold back on the fortissimos, but to hurl all my energy on the keys without fear of banging. Perhaps for this very reason I forgot about my apprehensions; with ever greater control I went from one tempo to another, passing from spirit to eloquence, from eloquence to fury and feverishness; the fever passed into sweetness, and then again into vertigo, then sweetness again, calm. At a given moment I surprised myself in the noble measures of the final lento. I had performed the sonata at the correct tempo, without the slightest clumsiness. And then I could hear, not exactly applause, but yes a murmur of approval, a breath. Someone had listened to the sonata with me. I felt certain of a real presence. I looked around: when I faced the painting, I encountered that radiant look of sympathy in Julio's eyes which only illumined his face when he spoke with my mother. Then I played the sonata again, but beginning with the third movement, the passionate, confidential cantabile. And while I played I threw my head back, watching Julio's eyes. Julio smiled like someone who has been surprised at a moment of weakness and understands right away that it is useless to pretend to the contrary. He spoke slowly, and the words didn't alter the tone of his voice, a soft, yielding voice which followed the delicate arabesques of the cantabile and induced me to respond: at a certain moment, it was I who was talking. And talking effortlessly: I spoke, obeying an impulse as spontaneous and imperceptible as that of a descending chromatic which allows the left hand to carry the melody an octave lower, and makes the accompaniment pass to the upper notes. I have played the Sonata in B Minor many times since that afternoon, and the cantabile of the allegretto and of the andante sostenuto has spoken to me in its secret language. But whatever its message, whether more or less prodigious and dazzling, the happiness which has possessed me has always been the same. I say happiness, yes, but there is something sad about that happiness. It bears within itself the anguish of its own end. We are enraptured and aggrieved by its vehemence. We feel nostalgia for the pleasure it gives us, and we regret, in advance, the moments of glory which it allows us to know.

I felt a moment of glory that afternoon, when Julio confessed his admiration for me. He didn't tell me before, so as not to encourage that excessive respect for my person which Isabel created in the house. Besides, approaching me would have meant struggling with Isabel, contesting her influence over me, conquering her. And harming me in another way. He spoke of "material things." I answered, a little abashed, that that musical talent which he recognized in me signified implicitly an absolute scorn for material things. In any case, from that moment on I renounced all aspirations of that kind: I had no aspiration besides music, or more accurately, besides giving myself up to the affection of Julio and my mother by means of music. I didn't desire power, honor, wealth. For a moment I made mine those hypothetical gains which destiny might offer me, in order to feel, on rejecting them a moment later, the harsh pleasure of those powerful, worldly men who consecrate themselves ardently to God deep within monasteries. Julio smiled. He made me see that music demanded certain sacrifices of me, one above all: putting up with Isabel. "Isabel has some good qualities," I replied. "Yes," said Julio, "but she wants to have them all. She wants, besides, for everyone to affirm her perfection. She distrusts anyone who resists her designs or tries to live outside them. She needs to be surrounded with slaves." "She likes music," I insisted; "she is a very well educated woman." Julio, without contradicting me, pointed out some traits of Isabel's character which modified my words imperceptibly: "She is a very well educated woman who doesn't scorn material things. Sometimes music grants renown and success. Isabel likes success. Sometimes I find her too inflexible; with poor Mlle. Lenoir for example." "She did

49

it for my sake," I answered; "if I were still studying with Mlle. Lenoir I would not be able to play Liszt's Sonata." At that moment I struck the final chords and the low B of the bass still vibrated in the air when I heard laughter and exclamations. I was held by the waist; a cheek was pressed against mine. It was Isabel.

V.

My dialogue with the portrait continued every afternoon. Now that Julio and I had broken the ice once and for all, we had a lot to talk about. On one occasion we spoke of our father and alluded, in a veiled fashion, to his marital infidelity. We exchanged reflections on how difficult it is to free oneself from dissipation once the habit of it has been acquired in youth. I declared that a dissolute old age seemed repugnant to me, even for esthetic reasons. I judged, also, that it was better to hide certain things when one hasn't the strength to do without them. Julio burst out laughing.

No, I wasn't praising hypocrisy. But a few days before, leafing through a file of legal records which my father had brought home to study at night, I had found a letter. My father could have been more careful with his love letters—although loving was not, perhaps, the right epithet to qualify that letter; on the other hand, the judicial file, the greasy pages of which seemed to give off a corrupt odor of a dissipate life, of filth and tobacco, was the right place to keep it. In the letter, which was written on the stationery of a cabaret, a woman was asking him for money. It was an ordinary, venal adventure. "What will my mother think!" I cried out. "Nothing," Julio answered. "These things can no longer hurt her. Isabel knows." "Why do you bring in Isabel?" I asked. Then, his smile gradually disappearing, Julio made me understand that it is difficult to hold one single person wholly responsible for any action whatsoever. So many people took part in it more or less directly, by omission or commission, that nobody could feel free of guilt if viewed in this way; at times, it acquired the fuzzy, intricate texture of a tapestry; at other moments, the encompassing clarity of a cloud. As if noting my surprise, he added: "I don't blame you, to be sure, for the

50

fact that they fired Mlle. Lenoir, but in the case of our father, do you suppose that his limited resources would allow him to maintain his family, pay for our education, and carry on a dissipate life besides? Someone has made that miracle possible, someone conscious of his misconduct, who used to be pleased by that misconduct and is no longer, but was earlier, when it could have hurt your mother."

The reader will have been mistaken if he thinks that my dialogues with Julio always dealt with facts. I don't deny that sometimes we started off from a concrete detail, but we immediately left it behind, and that detail, a simple pretext, carried us vigorously upwards toward more noble and abstract regions. Escaping from everyday reality, we found ourselves, suddenly, in a truer reality. We succeeded in explaining and surpassing it.

I insist that I talked with the greatest ease. And at times I didn't hesitate to consult him about certain circumstances which lost their improper, confessional quality by being said aloud. They stopped being shameless revelations. The obsessions of the fourteen-year-old rose up from the dark places in my soul, came to the surface, and then left me, and then, later still, I felt them floating around me, stripped of their dark, poisonous residue, of the bewitching power they had had over me. I recognized my former obsessions miraculously transformed from passionate crises into sharp, essential perspectives on the nature of man and his destiny in the world, which concerned me in a purely intellectual manner: not content with having freed me from a cruel slavery, these new perspectives struggled to follow my orders, to fill me with optimism and wisdom. Reason and passion, the spirit and the flesh, duty and instinct, so many contrary laws and irreconcilable elements (which still coexist in me) kept on and keep on speaking. But their rankling debate no longer deafened me, and I listened to them discourse one after another, with that tenuous lucidity which our words acquire in good dreams. Now, without having to respond to the Sonata in B Minor, our dialogue went on uninterruptedly, limpid, fluid, musical, bound to the clear melodic line which is divided between two voices in a certain andante in Mozart, or in Schumann's Romanza in F, or in Chopin's Second Prelude. And it was, par excellence, the dialogue between brothers: of an absolute, generic fraternity, as can only be imagined between two brothers. Of the kind which in real life, between two brothers, is unimaginable.

Of course that same day or the next I encountered a less communicative Julio. At table we sat facing one another. He seemed to ignore me. I see him eat lunch in silence and get up as soon as he has gulped down his coffee. He kisses my mother and goes out of the dining room; I hear his steps in the garden. After a moment, I hear the same steps again. Julio crosses the garden in the opposite direction and goes out to the street, after having said goodbye to his rats.

VI.

The rats were kept in large shelves with covers of chicken wire. They were white. Their fat, pink tails often poked through the holes in the wire mesh. Periodically the rats from one shelf were taken to the Institute and other, smaller ones came to fill the empty shelves; they grew quickly. The travellers were sacrificed at the Institute, to judge by the triangular crania, with all the little bones intact, which decorated the laboratory desk. The rats attracted me. I liked to go up to the laboratory at dusk. I heard them scurrying about, scratching on wood, shrieking. Alarming little balls of pink crystal gleamed in the twilight. Once the eyes of the rats went out suddenly when Julio turned on the electric light.

"What are you doing here?" he asked.

I begged his pardon; I was about to leave when he told me: "You aren't bothering me."

He went into his bedroom and came back a moment later, coatless, his sleeves rolled up. He took the rats off the shelves one by one and weighed them in turn on a scale. The rats knew him. Julio played with them, opening their mouths with his index finger bent to feel their long teeth: they never bit him. He also prepared their food, a white paste which he dried in the sun; after cutting it in equal pieces, he distributed it among the various shelves. This food had a smell which clung to the skin with an insidious persistence, the famous "smell of rat." In vain

Julio sprinkled his arms with eau de cologne after washing them in the single jet of the sink; as soon as he entered the dining room, my father—on smelling the eau de cologne—prophesied that bubonic plague would imminently wreak havoc in the family. Julio let him talk. Once, however, he condescended to reply:

"White rats are not carriers of bubonic plague; besides, what you claim to smell is not the rats but the food for the rats, food, I should add in passing, which is quite a bit more hygienic than our own: cornstarch, casein, salt, cod liver oil, and brewer's yeast. I see that you don't look too well; you should try that diet yourself."

But Julio added abundant water to that diet; they brought the water from the Institute in demijohns, with labels reading Avellaneda, Pergamino, San Rafael, Oran and so forth. Julio studied the noxious effects of various salts dissolved in the water, and had declared himself shortly before an enemy of aluminum. The aluminum salts had a progressively toxic effect on the organs and tissues, which could be corroborated by the fact that the rate of increase in cancerous diseases, from twenty years earlier up to that time, matched the rate of increased production and use of aluminum utensils. We learned all this through my mother, who forced into exile every last pot and pan of so noxious a metal. My mother spoke with that fervor which people assume when they explain things they barely understand. Flushed and enthusiastic, she made up for the poverty of her vocabulary with abundant gesturing. My father watched her with surprise; Isabel smiled. Then, as if to settle the matter, my mother withdrew majestically from the living room, returning moments later carrying some foreign journals which mentioned "the very interesting but hazardous research on vanadium and aluminium that Dr. Julio Heredia, of Buenos Aires, has undertaken," and the note by M. Gabriel Renard of the Académie des Sciences, which affirmed that "dans une certaine mesure, les expériences bio-chimiques qu'a faites M. Julio Heredia, le jeune savant argentin, pour démontrer l'influence d'aluminium dans les maladies des os et de l'intestin, ne manquent peut-être pas d'une importance relative." I remember Isabel taking the journal from her hands and reading the paragraph—which was marked in blue pencil—aloud a second time, underscoring theatrically the "certaine," the "peut-être," the "importance relative."

53

This oblique antagonism between Isabel and my mother was dissimulated by a lavish display of good manners and expressions of mutual concern. Nonetheless, a sharp observer began to note something suspicious about the watchful courtesy with which they treated each other. Sometimes they themselves seemed surprised at the peaceable, mild tone of their relations with one another; then, out of a feeling of solidarity with the past, they exchanged a sharp look, a phrase whose insignificance contrasted with the combative tone of ardor with which it was expressed, or became reticent; and then they as suddenly made peace again after having proved that the old rancor which had linked them so peculiarly during another period still persisted, deep, active.

Isabel ate with us every night. Claudio Nuñez joined us twice a week, the days he gave me a lesson in the afternoon. At table, my mother and Julio talked between themselves, aloof from the general conversation. One night Claudio Nuñez praised the painting which Isabel had hung in the hall. "It's a shame," he told my father, "that you didn't keep on painting." My mother intervened:

"I admire that painting very much," she said. "Antonio painted it before getting married; it is a self-portrait. And now it resembles Julio. How strange."

"It's not strange that Antonio and Julio should resemble one another," said Isabel.

My mother affirmed categorically, "Antonio and Julio don't resemble one another. I am speaking of the painting. Don't you think that the painting looks like Julio?"

I was going to sustain my mother's opinion, but at that moment Isabel, Nuñez, and my father stared at Julio, and I think Julio blushed; in any case, to escape from that disturbing mental confrontation, he turned his eyes aside and fixed them on mine. It was only for a second, but I guessed his violent desire for me to keep quiet. I had luckily said nothing, but I didn't need to speak for Julio to read my thoughts. My father's answer took us away from the topic. Trying to combat my confusion, I listened to his words: "Once upon a time I resembled that portrait, or thought I resembled it. Now I have grown old."

"Now you have a different expression," said my mother. "If you had

54

continued painting, perhaps you would still look like the portrait."

Isabel and my father asked two different questions at once: "What does painting have to do with the expression in that portrait?" and "What expression are you referring to?"

My mother ignored Isabel's question. She answered: "To a—how should I put it?—rebellious and optimistic expression."

"Yes," said Nuñez, "the rebel is optimistic. That's why he has energy to keep on struggling: he hopes to win."

"Well," my father concluded, "I abandoned painting because I had lost my optimism."

Isabel said to Nuñez, "You don't know how much I insisted that Antonio continue painting. . . . Even here in Buenos Aires I begged him to resume. I have always wanted there to be an artist in our family. Delfin is a case apart. Perhaps he ought to do something more important than interpret the work of others. That is why I don't want him to sacrifice all the rest of his education to music."

"A pianist is not merely an interpreter," protested Nuñez. "He is also a creator, or, if you prefer, a re-creator. Besides, Delfin could study harmony. I was going to suggest it to him."

Isabel interrupted: "I want to show you other paintings by Antonio, some landscapes. Sometime, if he permits us, I will take you up to the attic."

My father confessed that his paintings produced in him an almost physical malaise.

"But that self-portrait . . ."

"It is a sketch."

"So you prefer the sketches, the first outlines, to the finished works?" asked Nuñez.

My father clarified the meaning of his words by referring to his reactions a few days before, in the house of a friend, to a painting by the Spaniard Zuloaga. The design, the composition, and the coloring had frankly seemed poor to him, and yet, the painting as a whole repelled him less than other paintings by Zuloaga. He drew nearer and understood that it was the work of an imitator of Zuloaga, a disciple utterly without talent.

55

"When one takes a wrong path," he said, "no matter how much diligence and natural gifts one may possess, the results are ever more detestable. One sinks deeper and deeper into error."

But Isabel was committed to praising my father's painting.

"How absurd!" she said. "You had not chosen a wrong path."

My father admitted that he, esthetically speaking, had been very ambitious. But this same attitude had demanded sacrifices and struggles of him, which he hadn't had the courage to face.

"And to make these sacrifices joyously, enthusiastically. To have that rebellious and optimistic spirit which my wife mentioned and which I have lost forever."

Isabel thought of material sacrifices and struggles. According to my father, it was a matter of struggling against fear, inertia, routine, conventional feelings, clichés, all that is facile. The artist should live in a state of perpetual antagonism.

"You postulate a systematic rebellion which leads to solitude," exclaimed Nuñez. "And it is not good for man to be alone, as Genesis says. The artist should not be at odds with the spirit of his time."

"It would be worth knowing," my father replied, "whether what survives of our epoch is not precisely that which seems most contrary to the epoch itself. An English newspaperman has written that when sociologists speak of the need to conform to the spirit of our time, they forget that our time is the work of the few who didn't want to conform to anything. Yes, we already know what you are going to object. It is not necessary to withdraw from others, to isolate oneself. But in bourgeois society the artist has lost all function and must isolate himself necessarily. Perhaps the work of art is the revenge of the isolated individual."

This seemed an exaggerated and inhuman view to Nuñez. But my father referred to certain manifestations of modern music and painting. What was new in them, specifically new, was an inhuman, anarchic note:

"They are the artist's reaction to the hostility, whether more or less disguised, of the environment in which he lives. At this moment, this hostility is the only stimulus to the artist."

"You exaggerate," repeated Nuñez.

But my father spoke without a spirit of protest. He agreed, besides,

56

that every work of art carries a destructive element within itself. By offering us a vision of things which we haven't had until that moment, it proposes a new, incessantly new, order to us. Society, from its point of view, is right in being hostile to artists.

"You will not deny," he added, "that there is great hostility in its indifference. Better said, it is always hostile, even when it pretends to aid them, because then it protects dull or academic art; that is to say, it keeps on persecuting the true artists, though indirectly. It tries to crush them by every means."

"How unjust!" said my mother.

"Bah! The weak succumb, so much the better. In my case, for example, since I didn't feel strong enough for the struggle, I preferred to give up painting."

"Mr. Heredia took the side of society," said Nuñez slyly.

My father answered, smiling, "You don't know to what extent. I am an assistant district attorney."

The coffee was brought into the living room.

My mother and Julio played Russian bank by the fire. Isabel, my father, and I surrounded Nuñez, who played parodies on the piano. Bent over, fainting on the keyboard, he played a Chopin waltz in the manner of Risler: the waltz seemed a lullaby. Risler began to awake, to become contorted; he raised his arms to an extraordinary height, he changed into Rubinstein, and the waltz became a paroxysm of movement. Afterwards, we kept on hearing the theme of the waltz clearly, but it was accompanied in the bass by a Russian song; later still, the waltz was transformed into a study on the black notes, played at a prodigious speed; Claudio Nuñez had taken an orange from his pocket and made it roll down the keys.

From time to time, we heard the slight noise of the decks and the muted stops of the players.

Nuñez made me sit down at the piano.

"You two," said Isabel, addressing Julio and my mother, "try to keep quiet."

Julio stood up, and Isabel, who urged him in vain to stay, alluded to those inconceivable people who cannot stand music. They are truly pitiable.

"Don't feel sorry for me," said Julio from the door. "I have noted that music lovers suffer a lot. They go through life saturating themselves with impressions which they can only define by the vague pleasure which is produced in them, and they are always on the edge of sadness, oscillating between ecstasy and ennui. I don't say that about you, Mr. Nuñez: music is your profession."

"Nevertheless, a little music wouldn't do you any harm."

I swiveled petulantly on the piano stool, and said, "I am going to play Liszt's Sonata."

But Julio had already left the room, and Isabel, surprisingly, exclaimed: "No! It's too long!"

Claudio Nuñez, two days later, spoke kindly of my father: "He is well read, and has very strong passions, despite his appearance of *grand désabusé*. And Mrs. Urdaniz, with that contrast between her black eyes and white hair . . . A superior, absolutely superior woman. So civilized! Next to her we all look like savages. I, at least, discover to my chagrin that I am, at these moments, an immigrant in my own country. Your brother Julio interests me greatly. He doesn't like music. . . . Nevertheless, I prefer him to be a man of science and not an artist. I like in him the fact that he doesn't like music. That makes for equilibrium in your house. One gets along very well with the members of your family."

I would remember these words of Nuñez's on hearing the opposite comment. Cecilia Guzman told me, "What a family you have, Delfin! They are impossible to understand."

VII.

There was a certain Mr. X in Cecilia Guzman's past, a diplomat, who for a long time expected to be a widower at any moment and to marry her. About 1910, Cecilia lived with him a few months a year; the rest of the time she travelled to breathe the atmosphere of art in the smaller Italian cities, where currency exchange was favorable to the Argentines, or submitted herself to patient thermal cures.

I am barely acquainted with Cecilia's past. I imagine her, however, staring at her companion at table, the minister of a Central American republic, for instance, with a plaintive look in her blue eyes, wide open beneath the fleshy pink lids, while the gentleman slowly, with great dignity, subjected her to an optimistic prediction about the foreign relations of the civilized countries or—if he was an enthusiastic liberal professor, to a discussion of the last great socialist congress in The Hague. Cecilia had studied voice; according to the occasion, she offered her listeners songs of Paolo Tosti, Chaminade, Duparc, Fauré, Reynaldo Hahn. She was used to men in evening dress, with red and yellow ribbons on the lapel, some of them obese, who complimented her very ceremoniously by the piano and later, in the garden, when alone with her, allowed themselves familiarities barely compatible with their old age.

War was declared in 1914 and Mr. X became a widower, and got married. But not to Cecilia Guzman.

Cecilia went to the home of Maria Alberti, an Italian friend of Isabel's, who proposed to embark for South America. The entry of Italy into the war surprised the two women when they were already at sea. They arrived in Buenos Aires, and stayed in a hotel in the Avenida de Mayo.

Doña Maria Alberti was a relative of the papal nuncio and owner of a property in the southern part of the province of Cordoba. Cecilia helped her with her correspondence and walked her dog, an unpleasant, growly lapdog which had taken the voyage with them. In Buenos Aires Cecilia renewed her friendship with some schoolmates, among them my mother, and sang at two benefit concerts organized for the Allies. My parents had the honor of being invited by Maria Alberti to dine with the nuncio. In turn, Cecilia and Maria Alberti came to our house.

When the latter went to Brazil, Cecilia showed signs of uneasiness. Her friend the diplomat refused to support her. Cecilia mortgaged a little house she had on Charcas Street, spent the money, contracted new debts, and began to frequent my mother's company assiduously.

One morning I found her in my mother's bedroom. At that time Cecilia was a stranger to me, a woman in a black dress which let her arms and much of her back be seen. She wept; from time to time she interrupted her sobbing to breathe deeply and to draw prolonged sighs—

59

which seemed very moving to me—from deep in her chest. She was lying on a sofa, her head thrown back; long golden strands, loose from her messy hair, drew shining lines on the silk-covered back. My mother, on the edge of the sofa, gave her a flask of smelling salts, and consoled her. Neither deigned to look at me.

Some minutes passed. I was undecided whether to approach them or go out of the room. The unknown woman began to calm down. At a given moment, her eyes met mine. They didn't show the slightest surprise. I understood that she had noticed my presence—from the beginning.

She sat up partway, straightened out one arm, took me by the hand, and drew her face so close to mine that I could see my own face mirrored in the two round, liquid spots of her blue eyes. Then, pulling me off to one side in order to get up, she said, "You have eight reflections in your eyes, as is said in French of top hats."

I cannot circumscribe my memory of Cecilia now, just as then it was impossible for me not to fix my attention exclusively on her. The circumstances which surrounded our first meeting, that morning, flow out of oblivion, are mixed with the image of her I guard in my memory, and communicate a constant mutability to my impression. I think of Cecilia and I see once more the sofa where she lay, my mother's bedroom, the grey silk of the wallpaper, the balcony open to the street, the geraniums on the balcony. I see my mother get up, leaving the salts on the table, and I evoke, in spite of myself, the cut-glass flask, containing white cubes which floated in an amber liquid. My mother, when she moved, shook the sleeves of her dressing gown. The gown was loose and light. The shape of her body (which was not in contact with anything external) could be guessed at, burdened by a long whalebone corset which she didn't take off during the entire day, not even to rest a little after lunch. The material was supported by her shoulders and bust, and hung from there, as if from a hanger, in abundant, gratuitous folds. Her comfortable dressing gown didn't give her the slightest comfort. And it is curious that my mother's life was full of loose, languid folds floating down over the whalebone, of spontaneous bold gestures which concealed a rigorous foundation. I don't know whether this detail will serve to give an approximate idea of her character.

60

Cecilia's appearance was less modest. I saw her observe me in the mirror while she let down her hair. She filled her mouth with hairpins, then thrust them throughout that blonde, wavy crop of hair, which when all put up looked like it was about to fall down again. The movements of her arms—her pink elbows and the folds of her back accentuated by the black chiffon—made me feel ashamed. I had the feeling of being outside the room, that someone had surprised me looking through the keyhole. I went out abruptly.

VIII.

Julio occupied three rooms above the garage which were separated from the rest of the house by the garden, but the garden had invaded them little by little: the bougainvillea, the wisteria, coiled around the pillars to fall, from above, in a profuse, violet rain. Some afternoons after lunch, I sat with a book under the vines. The gardener pruned the plants, raked the lawn, accumulated soft piles of petals; they were the same petals whose coolness caressed the back of my neck. For the spring of 1916 was very bright and cheerful. So many green leaves, so many delicate tints, the warm radiance of the sun, the clear air, all welled up from a dark reserve of happiness. The October skies saw me cross the garden carrying a bough of wisteria very carefully so that the flowers would not fall apart; I came to Cecilia's room, and Cecilia put it in a glass of water above the desk. Above the desk, next to a color print which showed "The Ruins of Palmyra," were piles of souvenirs she had bought in her travels, photographs of famous statues and paintings, of politicians and actresses. I remember Ferri's white mane, the arched brows and excessive bust of Réjane, and I also remember the moustache of a gentleman dressed as a diplomat, his two-cornered hat decorated with marabou feathers: Mr. X.

We slept in neighboring rooms, separated by the bathroom. Sometimes, when Cecilia opened her doors onto the gallery, I found her reading; she had discovered some magazines to which my mother subscribed; in these incomplete collections, already a little old, she followed the installments of novels with negligent persistence, as I was

61

able to verify when I noticed that she was not disturbed by the absence of some issues. But these postponed issues, which I had to look for in the basement, permitted me to enter her room when the doors were closed. Cecilia, then, made me sit down next to her. She talked, asked questions.

She had formed an overly logical idea of our family, and had resolved to win us over by flattering each of us. But she always chose the wrong interlocutor in these cases. She thought, for instance, that Isabel had brought about my parents' marriage to give Julio a home; she took for granted my mother's gratitude to Isabel, her supposed protector. When Cecilia talked with Isabel, she exaggerated the merits of Julio. Isabel listened to her coldly. Then, resolved to break Isabel's reserve, Cecilia could not find a better means than that of praising her to my mother, in the hope that her words would eventually be communicated to Isabel. She would say: "She is so intelligent! In Rome everyone knows her. She always stayed in the house of Julia Bonaparte, the cardinal's sister, an admirable palace on the Trajan Forum. Maria Alberti held her in high esteem. Before the war, Isabel went there very year."

"Not every one."

"And now that she cannot travel, she lives her life dedicated to all of you. What a generous woman!"

"That's so," answered my mother.

Cecilia understood in a confused way that our family was not ruled by her principles, but she was too faithful to them (or too lazy) to bother abandoning or modifying them, and so she kept on stumbling "de Charybde en Scylla," as Claudio Nuñez would have said. To be more exact, she encountered three stumbling blocks: Isabel, my mother, and me. With me she relaxed for a moment. I found her, then, less sure of herself than usual, full of intuitions and suspicions, in a state of mind particularly apt for freeing herself from her mistaken destiny and discovering the truth. But my naive answers drove her *da capo* back to her old convictions, and on seeing her return to them, ineluctably, I felt a slightly perverse, almost musical pleasure, as if I were listening to the third movement of a sonata which repeats, with slight variations, the theme of the first. Once, however, I was very imprudent. I had entered her room under any pretext whatever; I found her with her eyes closed.

She remained like that for a second; when she opened her eyes, which seemed bigger and more luminous than ever, I noticed that they were full of tears.

I asked her if something was wrong. No, nothing wrong. Just tired, maybe. In any case, I couldn't help her. She corrected herself: "You could help me if you were more sincere."

"Do you mean to say that I lie?"

"You don't lie, but you don't tell everything you are thinking. I wish you talked with the same ardor you have when you play the piano. Don't you speak with anybody in that way? In school don't you have any friends?"

"I have friends, but I don't talk to them."

"Yes, that's a family trait. You are all very reserved. But in that reserve there is a bit of egotism. Julio, for instance, ought to be interested in his little brother. I would like to draw you two closer together."

She added, "Then my stay in this house wouldn't be completely useless."

I burst out laughing.

"Why are you laughing?"

I don't know what possessed me to be indiscreet: "You have mentioned the only person who is really my friend."

"Who is that person?"

"Julio."

She stared at me intently. Then she said in a low voice, "I don't believe it."

"And I talk to him a lot."

"I never see you together."

"I talk to him every afternoon."

"But when? At what moment?" she asked me, suddenly annoyed. "In the afternoon you practice the piano and he's out of the house."

Julio was about to be surprised *in flagrante delicto* of ubiquity. I stopped myself. Several days later, while I was practicing a piece by Grieg, I remembered Cecilia, and asked Julio for his opinion. "I don't have any," he replied. "She is an inconsistent person."

It was an unsatisfactory conversation because I insisted on talking about Cecilia, and Julio, proving his excellent musical sense, pointed out some errors in my playing—especially one passage which I was playing at the wrong tempo. I returned to the other topic. This time I thought I understood that Julio was talking of love; Cecilia was my first love and I shouldn't be distressed by that; all first loves are a bit banal. Reference was made to the flowers I cut for Cecilia in the garden and the magazines I hunted for in the basement, magazines she never read. I spoke of Cecilia's sorrow; I had found her crying. Julio put me on guard against the unlimited cult of suffering. A person can feel sad for reasons as nonexistent as he himself: that is not sufficient to make us interest ourselves in him. Finally we reached a kind of accord: we agreed that good manners are a form of morality. From the moment that woman came to live with us, we had the duty to make her stay in our house bearable. "Well, I will try to be more attentive," said Julio. "But never—do you hear?—never again shall we talk of Cecilia. The topic bores me, makes our conversation trite, and I note in passing that it has a bad influence on your playing. You play less well when you are thinking about her."

IX.

That night, after dinner, I asked Cecilia to sing an aria from *Le devin du village*. I accompanied her in an arrangement by Liszt for piano and voice. Cecilia had a deep, well-modulated mezzo voice; sometimes, to give lightness to a certain note, she passed easily from one register to another and sang the double or triple mordents of a lyric soprano. When I raised my eyes from the score, astonished by her virtuosity, I noticed that Julio, instead of going out as he did every night, was listening to the melody by Rousseau with bright eyes and lips half-open in a smile which increased each time Cecilia intoned the ritornello:

Ah! pour l'ordinaire
l'amour ne sait guère
ce qu'il permet, ce qu'il défend;
c'est un enfant, c'est un enfant.

I had the sensation of playing in the hall, before his portrait, and I couldn't restrain a motion of surprise when I saw him stand, approach Cecilia, congratulate her.

64

Everyone congratulated her. She sang the aria again. Her little triumph had filled her with optimism. My mother repeated a phrase of a character in Anatole France: "Jean-Jacques Rousseau, who showed some talent, especially in music." My mother asked if Rousseau's operas were no longer performed.

"*Le devin du village* was in the repertory of the Paris Opera for almost a century," Claudio Nuñez replied.

"I would like to hear it as a whole."

"I have heard it interpreted by a group of amateurs," said Isabel. "It is a very short intermezzo."

Nuñez explained that the famous *Letter on French Music* raised the whole population, wounded in its national feelings, against Rousseau. Rousseau maintained that the particular character of a piece of music is given by the melody, and that the language in which is is sung affects the melody: "He makes a series of observations on the French language, showing that it doesn't allow music to have melody or rhythm. It is an analysis very full of rhetoric, at times quite funny."

"But absurd!" exclaimed my father.

"And useless, completely useless. The partisans of bel canto have said the same about every language. Neither Handel nor Gluck, for instance, wrote a note for German words. Mozart's *Entführung aus dem Serail* was the first German opera."

While I was sitting at the piano without playing, Julio stood talking with Cecilia. I was not ignorant of the fact that Julio was fond of music, although everyone else in the house believed the opposite, but now he was not sacrificing his rest or his evening work time to *Le devin du village,* but to the insubstantial chatter of our friend. Or was it that music moved him to daydreaming, distraction, inertia, filling him with a kind of drunkenness which he could not abruptly overcome, returning right away to intellectual work? On one occasion I heard him say that music was the enemy of thought, and when Isabel protested, citing him the names of some scholars and scientists who found a stimulus to their labor in it, Julio responded, "Yes, especially Sherlock Holmes." Remembering this phrase of Julio's, I felt ashamed. I reflected on the fact that I always interpret the behavior of others contemptuously and look for pretexts so as not to have to recognize my debts to them. In reality, a word of mine had sufficed for Julio to modify his attitude radically. I was moved, but it was not necessary to carry things to that extreme. I didn't want Julio to stop working just to please me. I would never fully repent of having given form in him to a desire which would redound to his detriment in some way.

I stared at him intently. Emotion, gratitude, fear, delicacy, the most varied feelings must have been visible in my face, but Julio (entirely different from those characters in Balzac who decipher from an orchestra seat the most unexpected, illusory message, which reaches them from one of the boxes by means of a quick look) kept on talking to Cecilia, to all appearances completely charmed by her. He didn't take my expression into account. However, Julio, basing himself on moral and esthetic grounds, detested falsehood. I should add that he linked art to morality and once, speaking of music, explained to me why we are moved by beauty. Beauty is the external and visible sign of an internal and invisible truth (he expounded this idea at great length). All at once I thought I understood: in the dilemma of having to oppose either my desires or his own deepest feelings, caught between fraternal love and the love of truth, Julio had come to create a fictitious truth. At that moment he was expressing what he believed he felt. He was lying to himself! Julio's almost magical gift of being able to read the hearts of men and discern the hidden motives of their acts contributed to this process, which he extended, with inexplicable humility, to poor Cecilia. He thought that Cecilia would realize immediately that his enthusiasm for her was a pretense and, to deceive her, he had no alternative than to deceive himself. I remembered his scorn for all histrionic behavior. The necessity for an artist to be an impassible witness to his own sentiments—he told me once—is the paradox of the actor, which barely functions in the ambiguous glow of the footlights. At last, with that disinterestedness which goes with true spiritual wealth and which allows certain privileged beings, by constantly surrendering themselves, not to drown in their own abundance, but to keep afloat, to survive, Julio did not content himself with molding his conduct to my desires: my desires were his desires. I had nothing to thank him for, since he had forgotten my entreaty the moment he satisfied it. He could be sincerely friendly and modestly generous. He made these reflections to me while I was transported with wonder, while the words of Claudio Nuñez reached my ears

66

like a contemptible noise. Julio kept on conversing with Cecilia. They drew away from us, went out on the terrace, came back in again. Cecilia leaned her head against the door frame, with that faded and slightly affected grace which she always assumed. She removed a bouquet of flowers from her shoulder, took it apart, and gave Julio a rose. Some jasmine blossoms fell to the floor. At that moment I surprised an ironic sparkle in Julio's eyes. Perhaps Cecilia was trying to draw us closer together, perhaps she was reproaching Julio for not paying enough attention to his little brother. With the pretext of picking up the jasmine blossoms I walked towards them.

"Poor thing," said Cecilia. "It must suffer a lot."

"Little by little it begins to move its feet, it recovers its sight, and finally is cured."

"How can the same poison cure it?"

"It depends on the dose. It is administered in an injection through the skin, or through the mouth, mixed with the diet."

"And what did you say is the name of the poison?"

"Aconite."

"Do men have the same reactions to it?"

"Almost the same."

"How interesting! I would like to visit that institute."

"I can take you any day. I work in the Institute every afternoon."

X.

Now, after playing a game of Russian bank with my mother, Julio seemed in no hurry to leave us, and I had the pleasure of triumphing various evenings in his presence on the living room piano, playing the same works I had studied in the afternoon, before his portrait, on the piano in the hall. I should confess that Julio, on those evenings, seemed an unenthusiastic listener. Once, while I was playing the cantabile from Liszt's Sonata, the haughty sound of his breathing began to trouble me. Seated in an improper posture, his legs spread apart, knees up and arms dangling, one would have said that he was asleep. That is what my mother thought. When I finished playing, she approached Julio from

67

behind the armchair and patted him lightly on the shoulder. She spoke to him sweetly as if he were a child: "You are tired; you should go to bed."

Julio instantly opened his eyes: "It's very hot. I can't work or sleep."

I understood that Julio had closed his eyes with the double intention of not being bothered by any visual impressions and of feigning an indifferent attitude in order not to provoke comment by the family. For everyone continued believing that Julio, appearances to the contrary, didn't understand music at all. Sometimes I saw him talking with Cecilia on the terrace. A breath of warm air mingled with the music from time to time and made the perfume of the jasmine and the secret, impatient invasion of summer reach us through the wide-open doors. Sometimes, I heard the voice of my mother, who had gone upstairs with the intention of going to sleep, and spoke with them from the gallery. They exchanged mild remarks:

"Have you seen the stars? Who could sleep on such a night!"

"It's late. Isabel hasn't left yet?"

"She's going; we're all coming up to bed."

"It's time. Enough music."

Other nights they asked Cecilia to sing. Cecilia tried to blur those painful, noticeable moments when the human voice emerges from silence, because she had a voice which aspired to silence, or rather, which aspired to mingle with silence without interrupting it. Years later I have remembered the stealthy quality of her voice when studying certain modern works for the piano: *Ondine,* for instance, the first measures of which provoke in us that curious illusion which psychologists call déjà-vu. From the moment the right hand begins playing its chord, it seems to us that we have never ceased hearing it, and the happiness which invades us is, perhaps, the happiness of the chord itself on feeling that we are responding to its persuasive, languishing, and finally satisfied ancestral call. And in the Concerto in G Major, also by Ravel, during that imperceptible moment when the violins come in, the piano's theme, dispersed in a void of luminous waves, is converted into the eternal, ephemeral sound, which each person carries within himself, although it is rarely distinguished, and which humanity sustains through the ages. These literary digressions are barely related, God forgive me, to Cecilia's singing, so perfect, so balanced, with her discreet, infallible voice, which knew how to choose the right tone for every word, for every note, and to fill the impalpable medium of sound with psychological references, ideas, feelings, intentions. I understand very well why it fascinated Julio.

But I don't understand why Cecilia lost confidence in her voice, and, with the intention of pleasing Julio, taking for granted his absolute incompetence with regard to music, made us listen to a dated repertoire. For she had gradually passed from the Italian classics, German romantics, and French moderns, to songs of the Second Empire, which filled our house with emanations of the music hall. And everyone yielded to Cecilia's new repertoire. Worse yet: they prepared for it, encouraged it. While we were eating dessert, I noticed a general slackening in the conversation. Puerility, vulgarity, cynicism, and bad taste entered our house surreptitiously, and seemed to spread out like treacherous, ambiguous shadows against the smooth surface of the tablecloth.

It is true that my father at that time was in the habit of leaving the house after dinner—up to no good, I'm sure. In any case, my father is dead, and I don't want to judge him. However reprehensible his adventures away from us may have been, at home he always observed an unvarying intellectual correctness. But where was Isabel, whom I would have supposed incapable of putting up with improper behavior? Where was Julio? Ah, I don't refer to the real Julio who offered me the heroic stimulus of his friendship every afternoon from a grey frame. I don't refer to the being who had managed to unite in himself the most diverse qualities: greatness of soul, penetration, enthusiasm, energy, critical insight; in whom the astonishing growth of ideas was not a consequence of an unfortunate emotional poverty, and in whom the scrupulous cult of good, the intense practice of every virtue, never redounded in vanity and pride, by that mysterious transmutation of values which the Scriptures point out so often. No, I refer to the slightly deceptive likeness of the true Julio, to the everyday Julio. Well then, this Julio was a decent man; he irradiated youthful exuberance, moral health. Even the lack of imagination which could be read in his face saved him from a certain disorder into which more sensitive, sickly temperaments tend to fall, and which is something like the penalty they pay for the privileges granted them. I am thinking of Claudio Nuñez, who carried this refinement so far as to take pleasure in bad music and dirty jokes, like those gentlemen who mingle with the riffraff in the slums from time to time in order to prove how different they are. Once I heard him exalt "the genius of Offenbach," while Cecilia sang *La boulangère a des écus*. That night at table conversation focused on the Institute. Cecilia, who had been there in the afternoon, had words of sympathy for the dogs and rabbits, but was inexorable with the snakes. Julio, to astonish her, had done all sorts of feats in the snake house. He had taken a *yarará* by the neck, while forcing it to sink its teeth in a glass plate and deposit its poison there; later, whip in hand, he had walked among the coral snakes and rattlesnakes. "He put on some boots," Cecilia added, "but even so, to walk among deadly snakes with such calm! There are things which only men can do. Too horrible . . ." Claudio Nuñez, then, spoke of the ancient friendship which has always existed between women and snakes, from the Greek priestesses encharged with the cult of Aesclepios, and Eve in Paradise, to the Arabian dancers. He gave all sorts of indiscreet details.

"But where have you seen those girls who dance nude, covered with snakes? In Tunis?"

"In Montmartre," answered Nuñez. "And in Montmartre I knew a Russian who had an affair with a boa constrictor. To warm up its skin, she submerged it every afternoon in a bath of hot salt water. The boa died."

Everybody laughed. Cecilia asked him to be quiet and, when he kept on talking, put her hand over his mouth. Nuñez withdrew her hand, after kissing it delicately: "It died of grief, because the Russian had an affair with the second violin of the Lamoureux orchestra. The boa stopped eating, became jealous and sad. They are animals which are very susceptible to melancholy. It let itself die. The Russian remembered it with nostalgia. She would say, 'Personne ne m'a serré si fort.'"

Moments later we heard the musical transposition of these improprieties. Cecilia's hands traced curves in the air, withdrew, rested on a chord. Suddenly, obeying a whimsical inspiration, they moved to the right and drew forth arabesques of sound overloaded with notes, high, clear, mocking, persistent, as if the keyboard were never ending. She sang. It was a psalmody which gradually acquired clarity and volume,

and filled the room. Later, reduced to a pianissimo, Cecilia's voice knew
how to find the right accent of persuasive tenderness to justify self-
indulgent husbands. The refrain of *La boulangère a des écus* ended with
these words:

> Que voulez-vous faire?
> Quand on aime, on aime tout'même
> Il faut bien en passer par là . . .

Hours later I repented of having judged Isabel so hastily of late, because
I heard her make an observation which coincided with my way of thinking. I was walking her home, the same as every other night, and would
have desired that we never arrive at Cinco Esquinas. Yes, I would have
wanted to walk on forever, to hear eternally the sound of our steps on
the quiet street. It seemed a preferable sound to music, and moved me.
I observed the sleepy houses, the erect and humble trees whose foliage
was lost in the darkness. A pitiful white dog scratched about in a gar-
bage heap. I thought about the strange trust we can have in inanimate
things, in trees, in animals. Three blocks farther along, when we
turned the corner by the Miro Palace, my eyes became moist when we
met the woman who fed the neighborhood cats. There she was, the
same as every other night, leaning on an iron fence, with her knife and a
great bundle of scraps of meat. What a good woman, I thought to myself. But I said aloud, to subdue the grateful meows: "How strange!"

And Isabel, who didn't bother to look at the woman, limiting herself
to frightening away the cats with her cane, answered, "Julio's enthusiasm for singing is very strange. And to think that your mother
enjoys living with that whore."

Sometimes, when she spoke a word of this kind, she took on a
dreamy air and pronounced it slowly, pausing slightly between the syl-
lables, as if wanting to retain it on her lips and forget the person or
thing denoted, in order to meditate on its absolute, general meaning; as
if thinking, "What an admirable word! It is truly the supreme term,
the flower of the language."

The memory of her father must have influenced the suspended, almost mystical intonation with which she pronounced bad words. I understand that Delfin Heredia was very alert to the voluptuous quality of
insults.

XI.

Isabel expressed scorn in many different ways. With Cecilia she chose one of the most deceptive forms: excessive friendliness. All of a sudden, as if she had discovered the merits of our friend, she lavished her with all kinds of praise and forced her not only to sing, but to repeat her songs over and over. I was disconcerted. Would we listen to operettas and little music hall melodies night after night until the day of judgment? Claudio Nuñez, who always agreed with Isabel, justified this sudden enthusiasm with arguments. Mrs. Urdaniz was right. Cecilia, like the great singers, kept her lips still and enunciated with astonishing clarity. She achieved a perfect tone because she didn't make gestures with her mouth, since all contortions alter the opening through which the sound passes, deforming it. In operettas, in light songs, Cecilia's virtuosity could best be appreciated. That music which is adapted carelessly to the words, in which the lyrics go from extreme slowness to vertiginous speed, demands superhuman efforts of the singer. No longer of diction: of interpretation, of intelligence. How the singer is forced to work with the music, to give meaning to a text incapable of expressing anything by itself! The music hall was the true school of lyric artists. All the divas, the *Liedersängerinnen* ought to study there. And we listened:

> High society, high society!
> I would have horses with nice long tails
> If my papa were the Prince of Wales.

But I have never seen anything more incomprehensible than the ecstatic expression with which Julio consumed this nonsense. He passed his free time next to the piano, dreamy, lazy, still, oriental. My mother, meanwhile, played solitaire. Later, Cecilia and Julio would go out on the terrace, where they were joined by my mother. But then Isabel would call Cecilia, Cecilia would repeat her songs, and Claudio Nuñez would again applaud frantically. All of them seemed to forget that another music, Music, existed. Yes, I was disconcerted.

Things got worse when Isabel decided to play bridge. I believe that

72

the disgust cards inspire in me derives from the memory of those stupid games. My mother put up with them indulgently. Worse yet, Isabel always wanted to run the game, and her strategy consisted of raising the bid or changing the suit of her partner, whatever her own cards may have been, if he bid before her. Sometimes, seeing the dummy down on the table, my mother smiled: "Isabel, why don't you keep quiet? Look what you just did to poor Nuñez."

Poor Nuñez didn't excel in bridge. But Isabel, at the end of the game, examined the score sheet with her brows arched, and when luck favored Nuñez, she opened her purse, which was hanging on the back of her chair, and paid him in front of everybody (she always carried new one-peso notes). The bills remained on the table; suddenly they would disappear. My mother found amusing the speed with which Nuñez slipped the bills from the table into his pocket without anyone seeing him. Since we finished playing very late those evenings, Nuñez would walk Isabel home. As soon as they left, Cecilia and Julio would burst into the living room, and Cecilia would ask my mother if she had seen Nuñez putting away the money. My mother would answer that she had not, in spite of having watched him constantly. Nuñez was a magician.

But I was consoled by the fact that they paid me when I won. Seated at the piano behind us, Cecilia would sing softly so as not to bother us. Sometimes it was impossible to tell whether she was singing or talking with Julio, because she passed into a deeper than normal register, in which her voice lost color and took on a confidential character. Long pauses separated each chord. When I turned my head, Cecilia and Julio had left the room. Then I would check to see how many points we were away from the rubber, and played well or badly depending on whether we or our opponents were winning, in order to finish off the game. My impatience was contagious. My mother, to be sure, played in a more distant and perfect manner than ever; she didn't even bother to tap the table or arch her brows when Isabel or Nuñez stalled with cards in hand. But I felt her uneasiness. One night she asked: "Where are Cecilia and Julio?"

"On the terrace."

She called them. They didn't answer.

"They have probably gone down to the garden."

73

Half an hour later, when she saw them come in, my mother said, "Well, the last hand. We are going to bed later and later."

The next night she refused to play. Cecilia replaced her for a week, but Isabel's enthusiasm for cards was diminishing. We slowly returned to our old habits. After dinner they asked me to play the piano again; after dinner Julio would again leave as soon as the music started. He seemed desirous of making up for lost time; it seemed also that his intimacy with Cecilia was not destined to prosper. Suddenly, Cecilia began to withdraw, to get smaller, to enter that confused, grey region where all of us (except my mother) were jumbled together in Julio's eyes. On the other hand, Julio renewed his conversation with my mother in the garden and even got into the habit, when we were at table, of taking her by the hand, a rather surprising gesture for such an undemonstrative man. Cecilia resigned herself to Julio's new attitude; with a greater tact than I would have thought her capable of, she made no effort to hold onto him, and I almost dare say that now she fled his presence. About that time Isabel discovered that singing made her tired. Mrs. Urdaniz was right, explained Nuñez. Singing is the least musical form of music, because it is the least impersonal. Ultimately, what we search for in music is a representation of the cosmos before man existed, a little orgy of the infinite. In singing there is an excessive, disproportionate human element. Finally Cecilia found very few occasions to perform. I felt myself constrained to ask her to sing, and sometimes I even came to play on the piano those same Offenbach or Gilbert and Sullivan operettas. Thinking it over, they were quite innocent.

"I don't understand," Cecilia would say, "why you want to hear those songs, if basically you can't stand them. You have very austere taste. Julio says that it is a question of age."

"Have you talked with Julio about me?"

This scene repeated itself. I claimed that the songs amused me.

"If they amuse you, so much the worse. As Julio says, you are too young to like bad music. Isabel has already asked me not to sing. Can you guess why?"

"No."

"According to Julio, she is afraid that you will be corrupted."

"Don't be silly."

74

"Jul—"

She interrupted herself: "—everyone has noticed."

Another night we were sitting at table without waiting for Julio. Cecilia looked older. After observing her for a moment by the lamplight, I came to the conclusion that she had put on more makeup than usual. Cosmetics at that time didn't lend themselves to that candor which Baudelaire preaches in *L'Art romantique,* and women like Cecilia who used them lavishly had to stay alert, to smile, to keep a lively look, to blend into the pink, the white, and the blue with which they daubed their faces; that is, they had to use these tools together with equally fictitious ones of a subjective, vigorous type, in order to lend them verisimilitude. That night Cecilia didn't make the slightest effort. She was aloof, far away from the brilliant mask which occupied her place among us. Then they called on the phone to say that Julio wouldn't be home for dinner. The mask remained still, elbows on the table, a cheek leaning on one hand. She already knew that Julio wouldn't come to dinner. I understood it instinctively, and also understood, among other things, why Julio's name came to Cecilia's lips in spite of herself, why Julio and Cecilia seemed to avoid one another, hardly speaking in public. "They talk when they are alone," I thought, with a feeling of confusion arising from the memory of a question Cecilia had asked me: "When? At what moment?" And now I went on repeating the question. Imperturbable, ill-willed, keen-sighted.

XII.

My father's turn to serve in court came that January and we couldn't leave Buenos Aires. The night that Julio ate out, I accompanied Isabel, same as always. On my return I met up with Julio, who had just arrived from the Institute and was talking with my mother. An overpowering fragrance emanated from the snow-white gardenia bushes, half-hidden by the railing of the stairs to the garden.

And the smell of gardenias rose up to my room, and must have wrapped me in their unhealthy, narcotic exhalations. I was asleep; nonetheless, I didn't lose consciousness of being asleep. A cold glow lit

75

up the shadows, and the furniture emerged from the penumbra to offer its clear straight lines, its dense grey planes, to that soft, general accompaniment. I remember the intense feeling of relief which the darkness gave me when I was able to open my eyes, and the mosquito net brushing against my face when I was able to sit up. I got up, walked a few steps, leaned my face against the wooden blinds for a moment, and opened the blinds.

Then I smelled the gardenias again and felt underfoot, in the middle of the night, the warmth of the mosaics, which still preserved the afternoon sun. In the gallery, the huge shadows of the trees in the plaza came ever nearer, and the plants in the garden, the invisible flowers, mixed their exalted, vegetal breath with my breath. That night and other nights, at the end of the gallery where I had to take refuge because of a sudden illumination, I saw two diamond-shaped stained-glass windows light up; then I saw Cecilia's blinds half-open, and the light go out. Then, more than seeing, I guessed at the silhouette of a man who walked toward the servants' staircase. I followed him very slowly, like a protective genie, fearful that someone might see him. We were, so to speak, a single human presence advancing among the night breezes. From above, immobile, I waited for the silhouette to cross the garden before returning to my bedroom. Perhaps both of us fell into bed simultaneously, and at the same moment closed our eyes and plunged into sleep.

Ah, those strange, passionate January nights. The next day I looked with astonishment at the gallery, the garden, the trees, reduced to their strict limits, impoverished by the sunlight. There was a certain deliberate, almost theatrical, innocence in the impartial aspect with which they received me every morning. Hadn't the night left its traces on them? For it continued weighing on me. Julio's gestures and words led me irrevocably back to the night. And I identified myself with his gestures, his words. Once, at dessert, while Julio held one of my mother's hands in his, my own face—projected onto a glass door, among the lights of the dining room—surprised me like the face of a stranger. I lowered my eyes and observed my hands deformed by so much practicing, nervous, overly expressive, different from Julio's hands. From then on, my physical appearance began to trouble me as if it were a disguise.

Little by little I learned to brush my hair and tie my tie correctly without the help of the mirror. Ultimately, I was the only place where I could disregard and forget myself. I didn't look at myself anymore. On the other hand, from the piano in the hall I raised my eyes, contemplating myself in the portrait. I contemplated myself attentively, admiringly.

What a frank, generous face! The very portrait seemed surprised by its duplicity, or our duplicity, if you will. Because the identification which now existed between us had made illusory every attempt at dialogue. At that time I was studying a Prokofiev sonata, and my hands came and went about the keyboard in an arduous monologue.

In the dissonant harmonics, while I let myself be carried away by the limpid and strident mass of sound, I could distinguish the arbitrary combination of the perfect chords, and the cunning, odd use of grace notes and rests. I thought about Julio now and then, about what I called earlier his duplicity. He also was composed of many natural feelings, each one perfect when taken by itself, and which I now recognized as a tremendously powerful force when they were united in that duplicity. There was almost a virtue in openly defying virtue, with its well-established principles and its dogmatic formulas. Julio, once the night was over, recovered his candor, the same as the trees, the garden. Perhaps the trees, the garden hadn't intervened in the act of darkness? Besides, the desire not to hurt my mother was present in his conduct. He mercifully deceived my mother; he freely mocked Isabel's clumsy machinations; he succeeded in conquering Isabel on her own territory, the territory of hypocrisy. And wasn't the desire to complete his triumph, by conquering the only esteem which matters to an intelligent man, the esteem of the adversary, what made me awake Isabel's suspicions? At first I thought I had acted in that way absent-mindedly. I should confess that I have a special indulgence for absent-minded people; their forgetfulness and mistakes move me instead of making me impatient, and I am ready to excuse Tiberius Claudius for all the (perhaps fictitious) crimes of which Suetonius accuses him for having asked, when he sat down at table shortly after having his wife executed, "Why doesn't the empress come?" Nonetheless, it is too easy to attribute my words that evening to simple distraction. In these pages I am writing I propose

77

never to favor my own character, not even with a fault. Isabel once told me that one of the practices which most repelled Father Hyacinthe, when he was in seminary in Flavigny, was a ceremony to which the novices had to submit themselves the night before ordination. The novice accused himself publicly of his sins; if he left any out of his declaration, those who had been his confidants, witnesses, or accomplices, cried them aloud and spat in the face of the guilty one. Well then, I would require readers conscious of the motives of my acts, insightful, just, fierce, almost divine readers, who wouldn't hesitate to spit at me if I were to lie. That is why these pages will never be published. But perhaps we never truly lie. Perhaps truth is so rich, so ambiguous, and dominates our modest human inquiries from so far away, that all interpretations are interchangeable and, to honor truth, the best we can do is to desist from the harmless aim of reaching it. In any case, I don't know whether I spoke absent-mindedly or deliberately, but at a given moment, when Isabel returned to her favorite topic and observed, with a certain bitterness, Julio's loss of interest in singing, I found myself making some rather confused remarks about the trees in Lavalle Plaza (which we were then crossing). We were passing alongside the trees; nonetheless they seemed so much more accessible when seen at night from the gallery! At night things seemed closer.

"But it is night now," said Isabel. "What time are you talking about?"

And as we were coming to a lamppost, she blew open the cover of a little gold watch which she wore on a chain around her neck. She drew it near her eyes, and insisted: "It's eleven. What time are you talking about?"

I murmured in a colorless voice, "Later."

Isabel stopped. Suddenly she waved her cane in the air. She seemed to be aiming downward blows at an invisible assailant; she seemed crazy.

She was signalling a cab.

"It's too hot to keep on walking," she said. And when we came to Cinco Esquinas she kissed my forehead, and wouldn't let me get out: "You go home in the same car, and go straight to bed and sleep. I don't like your talking nonsense."

78

XIII.

It was late January and we were getting ready to pass the rest of the summer in a country house which Isabel had in Las Flores. That Sunday I went with Isabel and my mother to get acquainted with the place. We took an eight o'clock train from Constitution Station; after a three-hour trip, Isabel pointed out some casuarina trees from the window: "There's the house," she said.

I felt greatly relieved.

A coach awaited us at the station. Another trip, this time half an hour long, before we came under the casuarina trees we had seen from the train. In front of the house some dahlias languished in the burning sun. There were piles of iron-frame beds, tables, chests of drawers, and chairs inside. On the walls large rectangles were visible where the flowered wallpaper had not faded, which still displayed mysterious, dirty posters with Latin verses. Isabel took one of them down with her cane.

"They are souvenirs of the priests," she said.

The property bordered on a Jesuit residence. The Jesuits had rented it for six years and established a seminary in it. When the lease was up they wanted to buy it, but were unable to agree with Isabel about the price. They made her various offers. The negotiations lasted almost two months; they were about to be resolved when the Jesuits bought forty acres on the other side of the railroad tracks, and abruptly moved out. On these forty acres they had begun to build a seminary. I found all this out from the caretaker, a very talkative man. I had begun reading Shaw's *The Perfect Wagnerite* on the train; after lunch I took the book with me to the orchard and lay down in the shadow of some apricot and plum trees. The orchards reached to the edge of the railroad. To my right, above the casuarina trees, the baroque cupola of the church appeared.

When I went back to the house I found my mother with a notebook in her lap, writing. Isabel was dictating to her a list of things which it was essential to bring from the city. It was a very long list.

Afterwards the village painter arrived and had a long conversation with Isabel. They talked, among other things, about an upright piano which the schoolteacher could rent us. At dusk we got into the same coach which had brought us, accompanied by the caretaker's helper and several baskets of fruit. We took the train. Isabel had had a sleeping compartment reserved for us. My mother appeared dispirited. The property was full of old junk, there wasn't a stick of furniture which would do, it was necessary to paint it, clean it up; it was impossible to live there within the week. But Isabel answered every one of my mother's objections with the monotony of a madwoman: "The first of February it will be ready." My mother even burst out laughing. Isabel observed that I was very thin and that the climate at Las Flores would have a positive effect on my health. Not in vain had the Jesuits, who were such lucid, such prudent men, established a seminary in Las Flores. Yes, it was the ideal climate for thin boys, and I would lose my appearance of a hungry dog after a week at Las Flores. The word hungry must have suggested to her the idea of sending me to the dining car. They were very tired; they would eat a little fruit in the compartment. Besides, they had to talk about other things. She directed a penetrating look at me.

The porter took me to a table where two Jesuits were seated: one a young, dark Argentine, very reserved, with tortoise-shell glasses; the other one older, a Spaniard, talkative, ruddy, with white hair. The older Jesuit greeted me in a friendly way and made conversation. When I told him my name, he asked if I was a relative of Mrs. Urdaniz: "She is a very Catholic woman, a great friend of ours." He offered me wine. Moments later he was astonished when I, answering his questions, informed him that I went to a public school, the National College. I explained that Isabel had resigned herself to sending me to a secular school because I needed to have the afternoons free to study the piano. I insisted on the abstruse aspects of the problem, but the younger Jesuit intervened with an authoritarian air and said that there was no such problem, because in the College of Our Savior there was an excellent music teacher, Father Atienza, and even if I had to go to class both mornings and afternoons, I would always find time to practice in the college itself. The older Jesuit softened his companion's words, adding that music was not incompatible with a pious education. He would talk to Isabel about the matter. And he filled my cup with wine. With the movement of the train, which sped along very fast, the electric light on our table slipped over, and was about to tip over my cup. Then I took *The Perfect Wagnerite* out of my pocket and put it in front of the lamp, to hold it still. The younger Jesuit took the book, looked at the title, and passed it to his elder without saying a word; the latter put it down again next to the lamp, lamenting that Mrs. Urdaniz's nephew found pleasure in Protestant literature. But I explained that Bernard Shaw wasn't English but Irish, and added that he was a pious author, a defender of the Catholic faith. The older Jesuit seemed satisfied and told me that even if he had been English it wouldn't have mattered, because the Church had friends everywhere. When we finished eating, the two Jesuits got up. The older one gave me a little medal of San Luis Gonzaga, patron of young people, commending me to preserve my purity and to pray every night. "Very soon," he said, "you will have news of me."

I wanted to read, but after a moment I noticed that in the glass of the little window the pink hollow of the lamp, an arm, a hand, and the book were reflected. Then, pricking up courage, I resolved to look at my face. I am Delfin Heredia, I thought. I cannot deny it.

My cheeks were burning.

We arrived home after eleven; nobody was waiting up for us. Tired out by the day in the country and by the wine on the train, I fell asleep immediately and dreamed of the farm in Las Flores. In the dream my mother, seduced by the qualities of the property, wanted us to go there that very night. I protested, "But in the train you said the very opposite." "Isabel has convinced me," my mother answered. I begged for us to wait until the following day because I was too tired to get up. "No, right now," my mother answered. When I replied that there were no more trains at that hour, she replied, "That doesn't matter; we will go in a horse-drawn carriage; horses, despite all appearances, are very fast. Isabel and your piano teacher will accompany us." "We are taking Nuñez?" I asked. "Who is talking about Nuñez?" my mother answered. "Your new piano teacher, Father Atienza!" I asked her if she had gone crazy, and she answered that I was the crazy one, for not having the proper respect for my mother, but she forgave me because she understood that I was not awake.

A ray of moonlight filtered in through the blinds. I heard footsteps in the gallery and my mother's voice: "Cecilia, are you awake?"

A key turned and the door between my bedroom and the bathroom opened. I saw Julio go by; I saw him stop a moment, his profile against the light grey background of the wooden blinds. Then I heard some steps, heard the door to the servants' staircase open and close softly.

I got up after a moment, moving the handle of the blinds very slowly. At the end of the gallery a sort of very white waterfall surprised me, leaping on the open windows and running along the floor. It was my mother's lace negligee.

She was facing away from me, her head sunken between her shoulders, in the same place and at the same hour I used to station myself every night until Julio crossed the garden.

XIV.

Sweat poured down my back while I practiced sixths and thirds, or played the fastest passages of Prokofiev's Sonata at an unmusical, seemingly impossible, speed. I managed to suppress the noise in the house with the piano's racket; sometimes, when resting a moment and looking around, I discovered that they had taken apart a bookshelf in the hall or removed the armchairs. In that general disorder, among so many other things, Cecilia's steamer trunks and hatboxes were jumbled together. Our friend left one afternoon, allowing us to suspect that she would come back very soon. Maria Alberti had come from Brazil. Cecilia was going to pass the summer with her on a ranch in the southern part of the province of Cordoba.

At the table there were two empty places, because Julio ate lunch and dinner out. In the afternoon, when he came back from the Institute, he stayed shut in his laboratory until ready to go out.

My mother walked back and forth, watching the last preparations for our trip. At lunchtime she made an obvious effort to respond to Isabel's attentions to her, and the seriousness of her eyes, which didn't match her thankful smiles, moved me. She had the fixed expression of those who don't sleep, and was paler, more beautiful than usual. Her voice, her stance had acquired a melancholy dignity which corresponded to her physical features. I reproved myself for her beauty and sought refuge in the piano. I needed to confess my guilt in some way, to free myself, to prevent it from fermenting in my soul like a mold in a closed jar. Yes, I sought for an impossible haven in the piano. Music was no longer enough for me, that sterile monologue before the portrait.

The next day we were going to go to Las Flores. That afternoon I went up to Julio's apartment and passed straight into the bedroom. I observed the narrow bed and the mosquito netting tied to the white bars, which made it look narrower still. At the head of the bed, hooked onto a crucifix, another cross was visible, made of green palm fronds, already a bit yellow, of the kind that is passed out at church entrances on Palm Sunday. Over the bureau, behind the flasks, brushes, and a portrait of my mother, various cups of silver plate were lined up. I thought about the fact that Julio at my age was placed in a school in Ramos Mejia, and recalled that literature was exclusively represented on the shelves in the next room, among vast numbers of scientific books, by various volumes which contained the complete adventures of Sherlock Holmes. Until then, dazzled by the diplomas with honors and the transcripts which filled the walls of that room, and by the rats, the demijohns of water, the laboratory flasks and scales, I had never noticed Julio's bedroom. Now, with a certain slightly stupid surprise, I verified that there was a bed, two crosses, a bureau, a portrait of my mother, and six, seven, eight cups of silver plate. I opened a closet and contemplated an astonishing number of pairs of shoes, carefully polished and placed on shoe trees, arrayed on two bars extended at different heights off the floor. But through the balcony I could see Julio's shadow crossing the garden. I had time to close the closet and go into the laboratory.

I had decided to await him there. I vacillated, thought that it would be better to hide behind the shelves of rats, slip out once Julio had gone into his bedroom, and only then appear, as if I had just come. But Julio (I saw him through a crack between two shelves of rats) seemed to notice crossly that the door was open; he closed it violently, locking it with a key. It was no longer a question of having a talk with Julio that afternoon, that afternoon or any other, at least until the end of the summer. I resigned myself, then, to waiting for Julio to leave before leaving myself. I say incorrectly that I resigned myself: the truth is that I adapted myself joyfully to the new situation. Just as some people spend all their energy resisting the circumstances in which they find themselves, so I am always disposed to make it easy for my circumstances. I abandon myself to them, I let myself be vanquished by them—enthusiastically, lyrically. I am a friend of circumstances.

That afternoon I had been led by remorse to Julio's laboratory. An imperious desire for mortification, expiation. I remembered our musical dialogues of another period, and hoped to emerge purified from a talk with Julio as if from the miraculous waters of the Jordan. Now we were not going to converse, but to confess to one another. We would rival each other in humility, in insight. And the forgiving of our faults would come after having judged one another with the utmost severity.

A gesture of this kind precludes all forethought. It needs to be spontaneous, irrepressible. It no longer was so, and couldn't be so. As always happens to me when I respect the rhythm of things, I passed from one state of mind to the opposite, abandoning without regret a project conceived fondly in long hours of meditation. I understood that I obeyed deeper impulses than were possible for him who—having remained hidden for five minutes behind two shelves of rats, but now fears discovery—comes out meekly, seeking the right gesture. I could only free myself from the acts which tormented me by the same acts, which would themselves bring their own antidote, their exorcising and purgative quality. In even the best of cases, the imagined confession would not have been effective.

I made these reflections while the character identified with Julio took possession of my soul. Tomorrow, I thought, we are going to Las Flores and the portrait is staying here. I will pass two or three months without seeing it. I have the right to contemplate it this afternoon. Abandoned to my function as a spectator, I even came to forget myself as a spectator, having no consciousness except of the tall blond man standing before me, who was looking at a door with annoyance and in whom I was incarnated, perhaps for the last time. I saw him disappear into the bedroom; I heard water filling the bathtub and the sound of his steps which made the floorboards creak, the soft, clumsy, self-confident steps of those who walk around nude indoors, without suspecting that they are being watched. In fact, when Julio came into the laboratory he was nude, and carried the shirt he had just taken off in his hand. When he sat down, he rubbed the shirt in his armpits and tossed it away. Thus, before his work table, absorbed in thought, sweaty, sculpturesque, slightly fat, repugnant, he started whittling the little skull of a rat with a penknife. The damp flesh in contact with the leather of the chair and the hard surface of the table, as well as the shiny hair which accented the shapeliness of his chest on either side, helped fill me with that feeling of repugnance. Then I saw him grope around in a can for a cigarette; he lit it, puffed a few times, left it in the ashtray. He got up and came toward me. It was impossible for him not to discover me, but at that moment it seemed very normal to me, so completely had I forgotten myself. (The repugnance I mention above, which others seldom inspire in me, I often feel for my own person.) Anyway, the fact is that Julio passed by me without seeing me, and I watched him pass by without the least surprise. He took a jar of water out of the icebox, a piece of ice, two lemons. He looked for a glass, a bowl of sugar. He cut the ice and the lemons with the same penknife with which he had been whittling the rat skull, squeezed the lemons, and added water, ice, and sugar to the glass. At that moment there was a knock on the door.

"I'm coming," said Julio.

He disappeared; the noise of water in the bathtub stopped. A moment later I saw him approach in pajamas and slippers.

XV.

My mother entered the laboratory and stopped a few steps from the door.

"I have come to say goodbye," she said.

Julio exclaimed, ". . . to say goodbye?"

"We are leaving tomorrow."

Julio took her in his arms, kissed her. My mother turned her head to avoid his caresses, but he made her sit down and began telling her that he had intended to see her that very night, that he would never have let her depart without saying goodbye. This assertion was belied by his attitude of the previous week and by his recent surprise when my mother informed him of our trip. And the repugnance I had felt a moment before possessed me once more. I discovered a soft, ambiguous aspect of Julio's character. How can I describe the tenderness of his tone, the deceptive quivering in his voice? There he was, flattering my mother, making use of those unscrupulous, unmanly methods which are, nevertheless, an index of virility, because a man only acquires them through long experience of women. My mother stood up.

"When we return at the beginning of April I don't want to find you in this house."

Julio raised his head, stammering: "I ask your forgiveness. Cecilia was your friend."

My mother interrupted him angrily. "It doesn't matter to me that you had an affair with Cecilia. That's your and Cecilia's business."

She had sat down again, had crossed her arms. I saw her long, nervous fingers, with a ring I knew very well.

"I didn't think you were capable of pretending, of calculating. Similar behavior in Delfin, who is my own son, would have offended me less."

And I understood, as I listened to her, that my mother had come up to the laboratory to convince herself that a Julio existed who had been as hurt by his own conduct as she had been. Aren't we perhaps the first victims of our actions? And what else do we do, when we judge them severely, than come to our own defense? That is why there is always something laughable when someone begs for forgiveness. He can only forgive himself, and forgiveness only comes after that look of scrutiny which measures, step by step, the distance which has had to be traversed to commit the deed of which he is accused. Now, outside himself, from the just perspective which distance gives, he misses his already lost moral integrity. It is true that he can still recover it painfully.

So I reflected with a feeling of great exaltation. And the exaltation, which allowed me to discern my own feelings with acuity, made me lose heart at the idea of formulating them. Then, as happens in those cases when we say something to our enemy, the only aim of which is to express the exact opposite of what we feel, I listened to Julio's voice, which was more than ever my own voice and which was, at the same time, as indifferent, as alien to my state of mind as the rats I heard moving in the closets, scratching the wire mesh or banging the wooden shelves with their thick tails.

"Once more, I beg you to forgive me."

And my mother: "But Julio, I don't have anything to forgive you for. If I want you not to be in this house when we return, it is because I don't want to see you as you are. In reality you haven't deceived me. I have deceived myself. Ever since you were a boy, I have thought that you would have other faults, but never that you would be a hypocrite. Thanks to you, I had succeeded in freeing myself from a constant war which I waged against falsehood. I thought you pure of heart, loyal; I thought you were my own son. And now I discover, simply, that you are Antonio's son, Isabel's nephew. You are identical to Isabel, to all the Heredias. Not even that, you don't even have the virtues of your faults. Because the Heredias, in spite of all, would understand my reproaches, are sensitive. You don't understand."

And my mother seemed relieved when she said that Julio didn't have any of the good qualities of the Heredias. A light of sympathy, of tenderness, passed through her eyes, when Julio answered her with the only words I would have pronounced in his place: "But then—what do you want me to do? To kill myself?"

"Goodbye," said my mother. "Take note that I haven't told you anything. Keep calm."

And still once more, before closing the door, she said: "Many things may happen by April. Keep calm."

Julio didn't get up to accompany her, and began stirring the glass of lemonade which was on the table. There was still a bit of ice; the spoon made it ring gleefully against the glass.

I appeared at that moment.

Julio watched me. Little by little, his stupor of the first few seconds yielded to a fury which lit up his whole face. I have never seen a face so inspired by fury. Sometimes his face was against mine, and when a battery of insults, blinding me, deprived me of its radiance, a hand took me by the scruff of the neck and the face drew near once more. I felt at once my abasement and his glory, his terrible glory, his supernatural splendor, and I prompted him with the same insults, one after another, which he directed at me. Finally I was knocked by a blow of his fist into the armchair where my mother had been sitting. The face seemed to draw off. Julio burst out with an insolent laugh: "Now you can go play the piano, and tell Isabel."

He drew the glass to his lips, but hesitated, set it back down on the table, and turned away from me. I covered my face with my hands, wailing. I felt punished as well as appeased, and I remember the feeling I had of appeasing myself entirely when I took a flask (I had noticed it a moment before through my fingers while covering my face with my hands), removed the cover, and spilled the contents in the glass. Then I covered my face again, and kept on wailing. My sobs perhaps attracted Julio's attention: "You're still here?" he cried out. "Get out once and for all."

And I went out, leaving him devoted to his task of weighing the rats that remained on the table, very quietly awaiting their turn to go onto the scale.

One of those rats descended the staircase, crossed the garden, and reached the kitchen. When they went up to put it back in its place, they found Julio lying on the floor next to his work table.

He had poisoned himself with a ten percent solution of aconite.

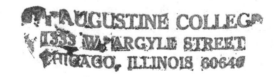